CLOCKWORK ALCHEMIST

The Thief's Apprentice - Book One

SARA C ROETHLE

Vulture's Eye Publications

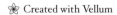 Created with Vellum

CHAPTER 1

A rhyen pressed his back against the cracked stone wall. He'd not expected this. He lowered the lantern in his hand as he glanced down at the aged corpse, then kicked it with his toe. It sounded . . . hollow. A pool of long since dried blood had congealed beneath it. It had obviously been lying there for months, but that didn't mean that who or *what* had killed the man wasn't still lurking about in the underground compound. Why couldn't the journal his client needed be somewhere nice? Perhaps an upscale mansion with a lonely, noble lady, just waiting for a dashing thief to sweep her off her feet. Or a cottage where an old man, childless and in his last years, would be waiting to grant a stranger the rights to his fortune. *Nope.* It had to be in a hidden underground compound with a corpse, that required a ten mile hike through the forest to access. He was lucky he hadn't gotten mauled by a badger.

Arhyen wiped the sweat from his brow, pushing back his shaggy, brown hair, then pressed onward down the narrow corridor. His boots, specially made to emit little sound when he moved, touched lightly on the stone floor as he crept further down the hall, holding the lantern in front of him. His client had claimed that the compound's owner had *disappeared*, but Arhyen suspected he'd actually been the dead man in the corridor. Had his client known all along? The journal Arhyen sought was allegedly valuable, containing a new alchemical formula for . . . something, but was it worth killing for?

He shook his head and continued into the next chamber, holding his lantern aloft to light the pitch black space. The stone room he entered was large, yet cozy, with overstuffed sofas, shelves full of books, a roll-top desk, and other expensive wooden furniture, all covered in a fine coating of dust.

Arhyen went straight for the desk, hurrying across the expensive looking dark blue rug that covered most of the floor. He gently pushed back the roll-top with his free hand, then set the lantern down on the desk's surface as he began pawing through neatly stacked papers. He had no idea, really, what he was looking for, so he would simply have to steal anything with alchemical symbols that looked remotely like the ones he'd been given as an example.

"Who are you?" a voice asked from somewhere to his left.

Arhyen nearly jumped out of his skin, skidding backwards away from the sound. He froze and contemplated his options. He'd left his lantern on the desk, but its light didn't push far enough into the room to illuminate the owner of the voice. He should simply run, but he still needed the journal, and the voice's owner didn't seem angry that he was skulking about. Plus, the voice had been female. As far as he knew, the old alchemist had lived in the compound entirely alone.

He cleared his throat. "I could ask you the same question," he stated bluntly, feigning confidence.

The voice didn't answer.

Making up his mind, Arhyen hurried forward and snatched up his lantern, then moved the light to shine in the far corner of the room. Someone was sitting in one of the overstuffed chairs. He hadn't noticed her at first, as she was in the corner, partially obscured by one of the bookcases.

Curiosity getting the better of him, he stepped forward. The girl couldn't have been more than eighteen, and wore a simple dress, with a high-cut neck and tight bodice, a common style. The pale blue sleeves covered dainty arms, ending with delicate, glove-encased hands, placed properly in her lap. Her vibrant red hair, once done in a proper up-do, was now covered in dust, with stray tendrils floating about her delicate face. She turned wide, blue eyes up to him to reflect the lantern light.

When the girl didn't speak, Arhyen cleared his throat uncomfortably. "I was told that no one would be here."

The girl seemed confused. "My father is here, but he stopped moving quite some time ago. I'm not sure what I'm supposed to do now."

Arhyen furrowed his brow. Did the girl not understand that her father was dead? More troubling still, was the fact that the compound owner was rumored to have no children. Had he hidden his daughter here her entire life?

He straightened his short, tan coat over his high collared shirt and waistcoat, quietly attempting to devise a kind way of explaining things to her. "Your father," he began, hesitant to break the news. "Your father is dead," he said quickly. "He will not be moving again, *ever*."

The girl's face fell. She turned her gaze down to her lap, straightening the white gloves on her hands needlessly. "What will become of me?" she asked finally.

"I'm not quite sure," he replied, feeling guilty, though he

had no reason to. "I'm simply here for a specific set of documents, then I'll be on my way."

The girl's face lit up as she turned her gaze back up to him. "Father has many journals," she explained excitedly. "I keep them all in order."

Arhyen didn't have the heart to correct her on speaking of her father in the present tense. Instead, he lifted a piece of parchment from his breast pocket and unfolded it. He handed it to her. "The document I'm looking for would have some of these same symbols on it. Have you seen them before?"

She looked down at the parchment, then up to Arhyen with a nod. "These are very special symbols," she explained.

Arhyen's eyes widened in surprise. "Are you an alchemist? Most would not recognize anything on that piece of paper." He gestured at the parchment still clutched in her fingertips.

She shook her head sadly. "I only know what father taught me."

He took an excited step forward. He'd been hired to find the journal, and wasn't sure what it detailed, but it was important enough for his employer to hire one of the most prestigious thieves in England. Prestigious in his own mind, at least.

"What is your name?" he asked. He knelt in front of the girl, putting himself at her eye level.

"Liliana Breckenridge," she answered simply, her face void of emotion.

Breckenridge. Perhaps she really was the alchemist's daughter. The great Fairfax Breckenridge had left a legacy after all.

"My name is Arhyen Croft," he said honestly, seeing no reason to give a false name. The girl obviously had no idea what was going on.

She didn't reply, not even with a *pleased to meet you*.

Trying to keep his frustration hidden, Arhyen tried again. "Liliana, do you know what these symbols mean?" he flicked a finger gently against the top of the parchment in her hands.

She nodded. "They're very important."

Arhyen sighed. "Do you know what they're for?"

She nodded again.

"Will you please tell me?"

She nodded, then looked down at the parchment again. "These are the symbols that father used to make my soul."

Arhyen stood abruptly, then looked down at the girl. Suddenly it all made sense. Her emotionless face. Her confusion over her father's death. She was an automaton. An artificial construct. They were all the rage amongst the wealthier classes. Fake humans, entirely willing to do ones bidding, no matter what that bidding might be. As a skilled alchemist, Fairfax Breckinridge had created himself a daughter.

He knew he shouldn't have felt bad, but he was overwhelmed with sympathy for the poor girl. Her creator had perished, leaving her alone in the dark to gather dust. Automatons didn't sleep, nor did they eat, so she'd just sat there in the dark, for who knew how long.

Still, he had a job to do, and Arhyen Croft never failed.

The girl's gaze remained on the parchment. "This is incomplete," she murmured.

Arhyen knelt back down in front of her. "Yes, this is only an example to help me identify the real thing," he explained. "Can you show me the original document?"

The girl nodded. She'd claimed her name was Liliana, but Arhyen was having trouble thinking of her as a human with a name. She was a manmade object . . . yet she claimed her father had made her a soul? It was preposterous. Souls couldn't be made. But then why were these documents so important to his client?

He sighed, realizing he'd gotten himself in way over his head. He should simply procure the documents, leave the automaton in the compound, and be on his merry way, ten times richer for his troubles.

The automaton seemed to be deep in thought, something automatons weren't supposed to do. Finally, she met his eyes. "I'll show you," she agreed, "but you must take me with you when you leave this place. Take me somewhere that's not so dark."

Arhyen inhaled sharply, but couldn't think of anything to say. He couldn't possibly take the girl with him, could he? He had nowhere to bring her, and he wasn't about to emulate the nobility with an automaton in his home. "Of course," he lied. He had to find the documents, after all. Once that was done, he'd find a way to convince the girl to stay behind.

She nodded and stood, brushing the dust from her dress, though she didn't seem to notice all of the dust in her hair. She was small, the top of her head barely reaching Arhyen's shoulder as she breezed past him. He followed without a word as she approached one of the bookcases near where Arhyen had entered the room. He held the lantern aloft to light their way.

The automaton skimmed the spines of the leather-bound books, finally settling on one near the middle of the shelf. She retrieved it, then opened it to reveal pages of handwritten notes. Upon closer observation, Arhyen realized that all of the tomes on the shelf were journals, not books. It must have taken Fairfax Breckenridge his entire life to fill them all.

She flipped through the pages of the journal until she found what she was looking for, then handed it to Arhyen.

Taking it with his free hand, he held the lantern close and observed the formulae on the page. Sure enough, the initial symbols matched those on his parchment, though the formulae continued on long after that.

With a smile, he snapped the book shut. Arhyen Croft *never* failed.

His elation was short lived as he turned to find the automaton staring at him, her expression questioning.

"You know," he began hesitantly, "it's very dangerous in the outside world."

She frowned and blinked her big, blue eyes at him. "I'm not afraid," she assured.

Of course you're not afraid, Arhyen thought. *You have no emotions.* "Well have you thought about what you'll do once you're out of here?" he countered. "London is a big place. You might get lost in a sea of people, never to return."

Catching onto his tricks, she crossed her arms. "We had a *deal*," she snapped.

He was utterly taken aback by her anger. Automatons weren't supposed to feel anger. They were *things*. Perhaps she was just emulating emotions she'd seen from her *father*.

Her arms remaining crossed, she tapped her foot, encased in a low-heeled boot, impatiently.

Arhyen sighed. "Fine," he agreed. He would lead her out of the compound, and perhaps she'd even follow him all the way back to London. Then she'd realize that there was nothing there for her, and he might even be kind enough to return her to the compound.

He placed the book under his arm, held the lantern aloft with his free hand, then led the way out of the room. A short way down the hall, he stopped and turned back to the girl following obediently after him. "Do you need to bring anything? Clothes, perhaps?"

She shook her head. "These are all I have," she explained, gesturing down to her dress and dainty boots.

Arhyen sighed and continued down the hall. Fairfax had obviously not been a very good *father*, if he'd only allowed his daughter a single dress. Automaton or no.

⚅

LILIANA FOLLOWED AFTER THE MAN DOWN THE HALL OF the compound. She knew they would soon happen upon her father, lying in the hall just like he had been for the past several months. One day she'd found him lying there, unmoving, and she hadn't known what to do. Her entire life had been *him*.

Now this man, Arhyen Croft, had arrived, and was interested in her father's notes. Perhaps he knew what she was supposed to do now that she had no master. Even if he didn't, following him was better than remaining in the dark.

Arhyen stopped ahead of her, and she knew he was looking down at her father. He glanced back at her with a frown. "Don't look down, okay?"

She narrowed her eyes in confusion, unsure of why Arhyen didn't want her to look at her father. She'd seen him before, not long after he stopped moving.

When she didn't continue onward, Arhyen stepped toward her and took her gloved hand. She froze at the alarming touch.

"Just close your eyes and I'll lead you past," he instructed.

She nodded and closed her eyes, used to taking orders, though she was still confused.

He tugged on her hand and she began to walk. Soon they reached the end of the corridor, and her hand was allowed to fall back to her side.

"You can open your eyes now," he instructed.

She did as she was bade, then continued following him down the hall. She felt a pang of sadness at leaving her father behind, but he'd want her to find a new purpose, wouldn't he? She shook her head. Perhaps not, but she couldn't just wait in the dark for all of eternity.

CHAPTER 2

A rhyen squinted into the sunlight as they exited the underground compound. The automaton seemed dazed as she stepped through the doorway, looking around at the tall trees like she'd never seen them before. Perhaps she hadn't. As the sunlight hit her, she finally seemed to notice the dust on her dress, and brushed at it almost frantically.

He moved away from her to retrieve his extra supplies from where he'd hidden them in a nearby shrub. It was a long walk back to civilization, and he was already starving. He pawed through his satchel and retrieved the sandwich he'd packed the previous day, when his journey first began, to find it an inedible mush. Scowling, he tossed the parcel aside and reached for his last apple, then filled the now-empty space in the satchel with Fairfax's journal.

He looked over his shoulder at the girl. "You don't eat, do you?" He instantly cringed at his own words, wondering if they could somehow be construed as insensitive.

She simply shook her head.

Arhyen bit into his apple with a sigh, then slung his

satchel across his shoulder. "I hope you're prepared for a long walk."

She nodded.

He wasn't sure if it made him feel more or less uneasy that she spoke so little. He almost wanted to ask her more about herself, just out of curiosity, but it would be ultimately pointless. He had no intention of keeping her around.

The automaton moved to his side and they began to walk down the dirt path that led up to the compound entrance. Yet they'd only taken a few steps when Arhyen sensed movement behind him. Had someone else followed them out of the compound? He casually lifted his arms with a yawn and glanced over his shoulder, just in case someone was watching them, but he saw nothing. Still, thoughts of whoever killed Fairfax flitted through his mind.

"Let's be off," he announced, turning cautiously back to the automaton, while keeping his senses focused on the forest around them.

As they once again began walking, Arhyen continued to listen, but heard no further signs of life around them, minus the cacophony of birdsong. He once again had the urge to speak, but found the idea of having a conversation with a manmade life unnerving. He grudgingly sealed his lips.

After just ten minutes of walking along in near silence, he couldn't take it anymore. They wouldn't reach civilization until nightfall. The thought of spending so many hours walking next to an artificial life form *without* conversation seemed unbearable. The fact that the girl claimed to have a soul made him feel even more uncomfortable, not less. She already seemed far different from any automaton he'd ever seen, but perhaps she was just well trained to act human.

"Have you ever been to London?" he asked casually, knowing it was a stupid question to ask.

She shook her head, unsettling a few more particles of dust from her red hair.

"Have you ever been *outside*?" he pressed.

"I'm outside now," she replied simply.

He shook his head. "I mean before this. Did you spend your entire life in that compound?"

She frowned, though her gaze remained forward. "No. I ventured outside many times. Father would occasionally have guests, and they often got lost trying to reach him. We would come out here to lead them to our home."

Arhyen sighed. So she'd been somewhat socialized. Perhaps that explained her almost natural behavior. Of course, automatons within the city were well used to social endeavors, and they still acted like blank slates, just waiting for orders.

She observed him curiously as they walked, as if waiting for more questions.

"What do you intend to do once you're in London?" he asked tiredly.

She abruptly stopped walking. She stared ahead for several heartbeats, then turned wide eyes to him, as if she'd only just realized she should have thought that far ahead. She was so still as she stared at him, he thought perhaps she'd stopped functioning.

"Never mind about that," he soothed, feeling silly for comforting something without real emotions, but doing it none-the-less. "We'll figure things out when we get there."

She still didn't move.

"Liliana?" he questioned, forcing himself to call her by her name.

A single tear slipped forth from her eye. Automatons weren't supposed to cry.

"I-I," she stammered. "I hadn't thought-" she cut herself off.

What had he gotten himself into? "You can stay with me until we find a place for you," he assured without thinking, simply wanting her to stop looking at him like that. What was he saying? He couldn't *keep* her. He raked his fingers through his messy hair and shook his head.

Liliana took a sudden, sharp breath and nodded. "I-I'm sorry. I should have thought this through. I cannot expect you to deal with such a burden permanently."

"You're not a burden," he comforted instantly, then bit his tongue before he could say more. By jove, he was an *idiot*.

She looked down at her feet, not taking him at his word.

"Truly," he lied, "it will be nice to have the company."

She looked back up at him and smiled.

Yes, he was a complete, and total *idiot*.

He fortunately didn't have time to shove his foot further in his mouth, as he suddenly sensed eyes on him. Not thinking, he whipped around. This time, he caught sight of someone watching him, though the figure instantly ducked out of sight behind the foliage. The face he'd seen had been smooth and flawless, without expression. A mask.

Not knowing if they had more than one watcher, Arhyen deemed it best to not stay and find out who the masked person was, or if they were after the same journal he'd been sent to obtain.

He grabbed Liliana's delicate, gloved hand. "*Run*," he whispered.

Not questioning him for a second, she took off like a cannonball, practically dragging Arhyen behind her as he tried to keep up. Quickly recovering from his shock, he gained proper footing and matched his pace to Liliana's.

They ran together, darting through the trees, and hopping over rocks and felled logs, until Arhyen's lungs burned and his legs felt like jelly. He did his best to keep fit, as a thief never knew when he might need to run away, but the long, frantic run after the previous day's travel had pushed him to his bounds. He was eventually forced to halt as his body gave out on him.

Liliana stood by his side while he panted and waited for his heart to catch up.

"You sure can run," he observed between pants, hunching over to rest his hands on his knees.

He looked up at her face to find she wasn't breathing hard at all, and her skin was still a perfect porcelain, not flushed like Arhyen's. Of course, what did he expect? She wasn't made the same way as he. Automatons were composed of flesh and blood, just like other humans, as such parts weren't difficult to grow in a laboratory, but they were profoundly different. The hearts that regulated their blood flow were mechanical. Not even the greatest alchemist could figure out how to make an artificial heart continue to beat on its own, so instead their hearts had gears, and ticked much like clocks, powered by the friction generated by their movement. Even movements as subtle as breathing through their artificial lungs provided power for their hearts.

"Are you well?" she asked quizzically, tilting her head to the side. The run had mussed her hair further, to the point where it barely held on to its updo.

He forced a smile, then straightened and glanced over his shoulder. Their masked watcher was nowhere to be seen, and he no longer felt eyes on him, but that didn't mean they were safe. "We should keep moving," he instructed.

The train station was still several miles off, so Arhyen

kept a brisk pace despite his weariness. He felt it imperative to reach the safety of a train car before nightfall. He
gripped his satchel protectively. Fairfax's notes had better
be worth the trouble. He glanced at Liliana, walking calmly
beside him. She'd claimed the formulae were for the
creation of a soul. If it was true, which he doubted, the
notes were worth all the gold in England. Alchemists might
be able to manufacture bodies, brains, and hearts, but
surely they could not create something as intangible as
a soul.

◈

JUST AS THE SUN BEGAN TO SET, THEY REACHED THE
train station. Liliana stood in awe of the sight. She realized
she'd stopped walking, but quickly forced herself forward
before Arhyen noticed. A few people were gathered
together on a wooden platform, glancing down the long
line of metal rails implanted in the ground. Though it was
true that she had ventured outside on occasion, she'd never
gone far from her home, and so, had never been to a train
station, though she fundamentally understood what trains
were. Surrounding the station was a small village, another
new sight for Liliana. She sincerely wished the sun was still
high in the sky so she could take it all in.

They stepped onto the platform together and waited
side by side. A few times, she darted glances up at Arhyen,
but he was too busy observing the few other people around
them, as if suspicious of their motives. He kept a hand on
his satchel at all times.

Suddenly, a loud chugging noise sounded in the
distance. She glanced past Arhyen to see the train barreling
toward them in the dim evening light. It seemed to grow
larger before her very eyes as it approached. By the time it

had almost reached the station, it was *huge*. She didn't quite understand how such a massive object could move on its own. She felt the need to run, but assured herself that if it was going to crash into the platform, everyone wouldn't be standing about so calmly. She forced herself to remain rigidly at Arhyen's side as the train came to a screeching stop on the tracks in front of them.

Catching her staring at the train in awe, Arhyen leaned toward her side. "Wait until you see London," he whispered.

Liliana shivered at the thought. She'd begun to regret her decision to accompany Arhyen when he'd first asked her what she planned to do once she got to London, and her regret had only grown as they ran through the woods away from someone who'd been spying on them. Now, faced with the prospect of traveling to London, with only Arhyen to guide her . . . she shook her head. She was a fool. She should have stayed where she was safe, even if she was alone.

As the final rays of sun left them, and night fully fell, the doors to the train car slid open. Arhyen lightly gripped her arm and guided her forward. She went reluctantly, as all of her thoughts were wiped away except for *one*. She'd seen how fast the train had gone before it reached the station. Now that she was venturing inside of it, *she* would be going that fast too. This was *bad*. What had she gotten herself into?

Arhyen slid casually into a seat, then gestured for her to do the same. He clutched the satchel with her father's journal on his lap. The thought of her father made her tense, but at Arhyen's warm smile, she found herself able to move again, and she slowly lowered herself into the seat next to him. Her father had never smiled at her like that, nor had his few visitors. They'd never even met her eyes as she served them tea and whatever else they required. She briefly wondered if all humans were capable of being as polite as Arhyen, then the doors to the train car slid shut, and she clutched at the sides of her seat for dear life.

Arhyen watched her with an amused expression. She gritted her teeth in terror as the train began to move. She closed her eyes for several minutes, then slowly relaxed as the train hit its top speed and the feeling of movement became almost imperceptible. She opened her eyes and stared forward silently for several minutes. Finally, curiosity got the better of her and she leaned forward to look past Arhyen and out the small window. She deflated in disappointment as her eyes were met with inky blackness.

"Feeling better?" Arhyen asked, drawing her attention to his face in the dim lighting of the train car.

She hadn't really taken the time to look at him previously. Such details were overshadowed by her desperate need to escape the dark confines of her home. Now that she had the chance, she noted that he was many years younger than her father, though she didn't feel well equipped to guess his actual age. His dark hair fell forward to partially obscure light brown eyes. His lips, now curved into a half smile, complemented an angular jaw, and narrow nose.

She startled, realizing she'd been staring for far too long. "I was never unwell," she said in reply to his question, then straightened her skirts beneath her and peered forward at nothing in particular.

"You were terrified," he laughed. "I've never seen someone so terrified of a train before."

She turned to glare at him. "Well, I've never even *seen* one before. If you hadn't, you would be terrified too."

He laughed again. "That's probably true, but it was entertaining none-the-less."

Hoping for a change of subject, she asked, "How long until we reach London?"

Laughter still in his voice, he teased, "If you were afraid of the train, I can't imagine how you'll react when you first see the city."

She sighed. "You didn't answer my question."

He lifted one shoulder in a half-shrug, though his smile remained. "Five or six hours, give or take."

Six hours on a train with this man, she thought to herself. Of course, she'd be spending even more time with him once they reached London. She hated to admit it, but she *needed* him. She had no idea how to survive on her own. Sure, she didn't need food, or water, but that didn't mean that she was okay with living out in the elements, with no human interaction. With no one for her to *help*. It was what she was made for, after all. To assist her father with his various experiments, and to keep their home clean. Although, she'd given up on that latter part once he'd stopped moving.

She sighed and mentally corrected herself. Realistically, she knew that her father was dead. She knew what death was, but she didn't *understand* it. She didn't understand life either. She couldn't comprehend that some lives were *real*, while hers was not. She felt *real*. She wondered, if *she* died, if that would feel real too.

Arhyen had turned his gaze toward the window, even though there was nothing to see except the blackness of the moonless night sky. He was *real*. At least, she was pretty sure that he was. He didn't like automatons either. She could tell that he wasn't entirely comfortable around her, despite his relaxed attitude and incessant teasing.

As she watched, his eyes began to flutter closed. She supposed it was getting late, and he had walked all the way to her home, and then back again to the train station. He was human, and he needed rest, unlike her. His hands reflexively tensed around his satchel, protecting it even as sleep took him.

Liliana turned her gaze forward, once again wondering if she'd made the correct decision in following Arhyen. She supposed only time would tell. With a sigh, she relaxed back against her seat and prepared to wait, envying Arhyen and the few other passengers their ability to sleep.

CHAPTER 3

The train's screeching halt jolted Arhyen into awareness. Remembering just where he was and what he was doing, his eyes snapped open. The sky outside the window was still dark, though he sensed morning was not far off. He flexed his hands around the satchel in his lap, then turned his head to view the woman beside him.

Liliana turned bored eyes to meet his gaze. Most of the dust had come free from her hair, though it was still a mess, and there were a few smudges of dirt on her face from their time in the woods. He began to reach out his hand to wipe them away, then thought better of it.

"You should straighten your hair and wipe the dirt from your face before we enter the city," he urged. "We don't want to draw any more attention than necessary."

"Why not?" she asked blandly.

He frowned, unsure of how to explain things properly to her. "I'm the sort of man who must remain inconspicuous, so please, just do as I say."

She instantly began to fix her hair, pulling it loose from

its partial updo to let it hang down nearly to her waist. She then set to wiping at her face with her gloved hands, but eventually he had to help her with the last few smudges of dirt. By the time she was presentable, the train's doors had opened and the passengers began to filter out into the night air.

Arhyen stood and walked past Liliana's knees to reach the aisle, then offered her a hand up.

She took it gingerly, glancing around in excitement. "Are we in London?"

"Not quite," he explained, then led her off the train.

Liliana gasped as she stepped onto the platform to look up at the distant lights of London. Arhyen smiled, thinking it was quite fun to show someone trains and cities for the first time, even if that someone wasn't really a *someone*.

A few other passengers still standing on the platform were beginning to stare, so he hurried her forward.

"Where are we going?" she asked as he dragged her away.

"To my home," he replied simply.

"What are you going to do with father's journal?" she asked.

They reached the cobblestone street and her boots began to clatter loudly as her shorter legs moved to match his longer strides. Did she really have to choose *now* to ask questions? The officers of the *Watch* at the gates eyed each of the passengers that had come from the train, asking for their papers before allowing them entrance to the city.

Arhyen came to a sudden halt, realizing one *big* problem with his plan. Liliana didn't have any papers. He probably could have gotten her some had he known he'd be coming back from his mission with a guest, but there was no way he could have had the foresight for that. Now it was too late, and he couldn't really expect her to wait out in the dark for several hours while he entered the city and attempted to rustle up some more papers as fake as his own. Well, he did briefly consider the option, but quickly dismissed it. Automatons were highly valued. Even if you could not discern one at first glance, any who might figure it out would gladly snatch Liliana away to sell her to the highest bidder.

"Come with me," he whispered, turning away from the gates shortly before the guards would have noticed him.

For once, she didn't ask questions, and simply hurried along, sticking close to his side.

Once they were back near the train station, they stopped and sat on a bench, as if waiting for the next train. Liliana looked up at him, her large eyes full of questions.

He leaned close to her side. "You don't have any papers," he whispered. "We cannot enter the gates without them."

She stared at him, a frank expression on her face. "You should have thought of that sooner."

It was so absurd that he laughed, startling Liliana. Her widened eyes soon transitioned to a glare. "I wasn't joking," she assured him.

"Oh yes, I know," he replied sarcastically, wracking his brain for some way to smuggle her into the city.

"Hello Arhyen," a voice said from his left, and slightly behind him.

Arhyen turned around instantly, recognizing the voice.

Ephraim Godwin smiled down at him. He wore a standard detective's uniform of a short, gray, broadcloth coat, matching silk waistcoat, and trousers. The lowly officers of the Watch wore caps with silver badges on them, but as an upper class detective, Ephraim had no badge in sight. "Did you find anything interesting while you were out of town?" he asked curiously.

Arhyen sighed. He wasn't in the habit of interacting with detectives, but Ephriam wasn't a normal detective. He was an investigator of the strange and unusual, and didn't allow himself to be fully fettered by silly laws if they kept him from discovering new information, and solving unsolvable cases. The Watch kept him around because he *did* solve cases, albeit unconventionally.

Arhyen suddenly perked up as he had a thought. "I *did* happen upon some interesting things. I might be willing to divulge them, in return for a favor."

"Or I could simply arrest you," Ephraim teased.

Arhyen waggled his eyebrows at him. "Yeah, but you know I'd just escape, then you'd never find anything out."

Ephraim sighed, then gestured for Arhyen to name his terms.

Arhyen nodded to Liliana, who'd remained silently sitting beside him. "An escort into the city wouldn't be amiss. I promise, we're planning nothing nefarious."

Ephraim stared at Liliana thoughtfully, his short blond hair reflecting the nearby lights of London, then turned back to Arhyen. He couldn't help but wonder if Ephraim had also realized that Liliana was an automaton, though the man made no comment. Instead, he nodded curtly. "Let's go."

Arhyen stood and offered Liliana a hand up, grateful for the fortuitous turn of events.

As the trio walked back toward the gates, Ephraim whispered to Arhyen, "It's her first time to London, I take it? Did you pick her up somewhere out in the country?"

Arhyen smirked. "How could you tell?"

Ephraim shrugged. "You get a sense for these things in my line of work."

He glanced at Liliana to see her taking in every aspect of her surroundings, lingering particularly long on any women or children entering London at the late, or extremely early, depending how you looked at it, hour.

They reached the gates, composed of metal painted to appear gold, though it was simple iron underneath. Liliana and Arhyen waited a few steps back as Ephraim showed the watchman his identification. The officer nodded in recognition, and did not question Arhyen and Liliana as they waited patiently behind Ephraim. Ephraim said his goodbyes, and the trio walked into the city unmolested.

Once they were out of the officer's sight, Ephraim stopped and turned to Arhyen. "I'll be by to collect my information," he glanced briefly at Liliana, "once you're *settled*," he added with a wink at Arhyen.

Arhyen sighed as Ephraim left them, then guided Liliana down the dark pavement of the street. As they walked, the sun slowly peeked over the horizon, bringing with it the city sounds of early risers, as if the sun had beckoned them forth with its arrival. Soon they left behind the small stone and wood residences of the border for the outskirts of the Market District.

"Who was that man?" Liliana demanded suddenly, startling Arhyen out of his thoughts.

"Ephraim?" he questioned, unable to think of who else she might mean. He shrugged. "An old friend, well, not a friend really. An old *associate*."

He glanced over to see her nod, almost absentmindedly. Her gaze was on the glass front shops around them, all still closed at the early hour. Her eyes darted about curiously, as if she'd memorize every single sight. She'd be in for a shock once they journeyed to the central area of London where the larger shops and cafes sold their goods during the busy hours of the day.

"Am I here illegally?" she asked distantly, then frowned,

turning her concerned gaze to him. "You said before that papers were required to enter the city. Will I be arrested?"

He sighed, unsure of what to say. "Ephraim won't tell anyone, and neither will I," he promised, hoping it would make her feel better, even though she wasn't supposed to *feel* at all. If she was simply pretending to feel, she was an excellent actress, because she seemed truly worried about the prospect of getting arrested. Realistically, she'd just be booted out of the city. Hundreds of unregistered citizens found their way into London every day. It was not a severe crime.

She nodded, but did not return his encouraging smile.

With another sigh, Arhyen led her onward, toward the place that currently served as his home. The smell of fresh baked bread wafted through the thin morning air, making his stomach growl. Traveling with someone who didn't eat had made him forget his own needs, but they were catching up with him now, overcoming his limbs with fatigue.

He glanced at Liliana again, watching her peer through the glass window of a clock shop. With a gasp, he quickly grabbed her arm to prevent her from walking directly into a street lamp. She stopped walking and blinked up at him in surprise as he withdrew his hand, then, seeming embarrassed, she picked up her pace and deftly walked around the lamppost.

He had to jog to catch up with her, covering his laugh with his hand. "So," he began, reaching her side. Though she didn't turn her attention toward him, he continued unperturbed, "can you eat?"

Keeping her gaze ahead, she allowed him to grab hold of her shoulders to turn her toward a narrow alleyway. Facing the new direction, she continued walking. "I don't need to eat," she answered softly. She seemed unaware of the piles of refuse and rubble around her, and didn't even hesitate as a rat scampered across her path.

Arhyen dodged another rat. Traveling through alleyways wasn't ideal, but there were some folk he'd rather not run into. "I didn't ask if you *need* to," he went on. "I asked if you *can*."

She stopped walking and blinked up at him, seeming surprised again. "I suppose I could. I've never really thought about it."

"Good," he replied, then took several long strides to venture ahead of her.

Her boots sounded on the cobblestones of the alley a moment later as she hurried to catch up. "Why do you ask?" she questioned, once again reaching his side. Her eyes held some emotion he couldn't quite decipher. Excitement?

"Well I could use something to eat," he said casually, continuing to stroll along.

He glanced over to see her thinking deeply as she walked, not watching where she was going. He'd have to keep an eye out for any more errant street lamps once they returned to the main thoroughfare.

"Would you like to try?" he questioned when she did not speak.

Her mouth puckered in indecision. He was prepared for her to say no, but finally she nodded. "Yes, I think I'd like to try."

Arhyen smiled as he habitually checked the satchel at his side. He really should have dropped it off first, but watching Liliana's reactions was proving too entertaining. He couldn't wait to see her try a pastry. Plus, he was starving.

He instructed her to take a right, then they were back on another main street. The smell of baking bread grew stronger as they approached a small cafe. Liliana jumped at the sound of a jingling bell when he opened the door for her, then stared in awe as they entered the establishment.

A glass case held a wide assortment of pastries and breads, all freshly baked. The smell alone made Arhyen's mouth water. They were the first patrons to enter the cafe at the early hour, though Liliana didn't seem to notice. She walked straight up to the case and stared, her mouth slightly agape. Arhyen came to stand beside her, noting the direction of her gaze. A giant slice of chocolate cake seemed to have caught her eye.

The cafe owner, an elderly gentleman with a kind smile, came to stand behind the case. "I see the young lady is quite hungry," he observed with a chuckle.

Liliana's eyes whipped upward and she frowned, seemingly embarrassed, but the old man just continued to smile. While Liliana straightened her dress and attempted to regain her composure, Arhyen ordered two cups of black tea, a scone for himself, and the chocolate cake for Liliana. The cake wasn't exactly a normal breakfast, but he found it a fitting item for someone's first taste of food.

They moved to sit at one of the many vacant tables, and moments later, the items were delivered. As the cafe owner walked away, Liliana stared down at her cake. Arhyen took a bite of his scone and a sip of his tea, then gestured for her to dig in.

Her eyes glanced up to meet his, as if needing more than the gesture for permission.

"You're a free woman now," he assured. "It's your god-given right to eat cake."

She took a deep breath, then looked down at the confection before her, completely ignoring her tea. She gingerly lifted her fork from the plate, then plunged it down into the cake. Lifting a single bite, she moved the fork slowly toward her face. Then, with another deep breath, she shoved the bite of cake into her mouth. As soon as the taste hit her, she looked up at Arhyen with a grin, then proceeded to chew the cake with her mouth open before taking another bite.

He found himself smiling, but quickly dampened his own enjoyment. This was just a bit of fun. Soon the automaton would realize there was nothing for her here in the city, and she'd want to go back home.

Liliana gleefully devoured the rest of her cake, not noticing Arhyen's change of mood. He shook his head as he ate the rest of his scone and sipped his tea.

When they were finished, he paid the shopkeeper and they exited the cafe. It was time to store Liliana somewhere safe, then go to meet his employer. The coin he would make from this journal would pay his rent for the next six months, and keep his pantry well stocked on top of it.

While they'd rested in the cafe, the street outside had grown busy with people going about their morning tasks. Ladies in fine dresses perused the various shops and entered cafes, while men in three piece suits passed by the ornate window displays without a single glance. Older, more distinguished gentlemen in frock coats entered the cafes along with the women.

Liliana watched it all curiously. It hit him then that she'd likely never even been around so many people at once. It had to be overwhelming, and perhaps a bit scary. He was about to take her arm and guide her forward, when someone bumped into his back, ramming his satchel and its contents against him.

He instinctively checked his satchel as the man passed, then his eyes widened in horror. The journal was *gone*. He turned to see the man's back disappearing into the crowd.

His eyes flicked to Liliana. "Follow me," he demanded, then he took off at a run after the man.

Arhyen wove through the growing crowd, seeking the thief. *There.* A black clad back jogging away, further down the street. He could hear Liliana's boots clacking behind him as the girl easily kept pace. The man who'd stolen the journal suddenly veered into an alleyway, and Arhyen followed right behind him. He couldn't make out much of the one he pursued, besides the black coat and bowler cap.

He followed through several winding turns in the alleyway until they reached a dead end. The alley was bordered by the tall brick walls of buildings on all sides, save where they'd entered. The man he pursued came to an abrupt halt, then turned to face Arhyen as Liliana caught up to him. Liliana gasped at the man's face, although it wasn't his face, it was a mask. The same smooth, impassive mask worn by their watcher in the woods. The mask's visage held a subtle smile, and Arhyen couldn't help but imagine the face underneath held the same expression. The masked man gripped the journal in one black-gloved hand.

"Return what you stole," Arhyen calmly demanded, taking an aggressive stance, "and I'll let you go on your way." He didn't reach for any of his weapons, not yet. It was best to keep them hidden for the element of surprise it would afford him.

The masked man shook his head, then leaned to the side to glance behind Arhyen. Once again, Liliana gasped. Arhyen peeked over his shoulder, then turned fully to face the new threat. Three men, dirty and dressed in ragged clothing, crept toward them.

Arhyen grabbed hold of Liliana and placed her at his back, then moved with her so she'd be between him and the nearest wall. The men closed in. Arhyen drew a dagger from a specially sewn sheath within his coat. It would do him little good. The other men appeared unarmed, but it still wasn't a fair fight.

"If you get the chance," he began, speaking to Liliana without looking at her, "*run*."

The men closed in as one.

Arhyen deftly dodged the attacks of first one, then another, landing a swipe of his dagger across the second man's back. The third pounced, and Arhyen ducked, then stood at just the right moment, hitting the man with his shoulders and using the momentum to toss him aside. The first two came at him again, and he managed a slice across the unwounded man's arm.

Arhyen smiled coldly, though he knew the odds were stacked against him. He was a skilled fighter, but all it would take was a single misstep. He didn't see Liliana, and could not take the time to look for her. Hopefully she'd taken his advice and ran.

The first man, clutching his bleeding arm, charged. Arhyen whirled out of the way, then gave him a surprise blow to the gut with his elbow. Liliana screamed from somewhere behind him. *Damn,* she was still here. Arhyen's eyes snapped to her, just as the third thug grabbed her arm. Without thinking, he threw his dagger. It landed with a solid *thunk* into the man's back.

Not giving him a moment to recover, one of the thugs jumped on Arhyen's back and wrapped a grimy arm around his neck. Arhyen spun around, struggling to free himself from the man. He attempted to maneuver toward the wall to slam the man against it, but suddenly there was a loud *thwack*, and his attacker fell away with a grunt. He turned to see Liliana with a piece of broken brick in her hand, and a stunned expression on her face. The man who'd jumped on his back was out cold at her feet. Footsteps sounded, and he turned to see the remaining conscious man fleeing back down the alleyway.

Arhyen panted from exertion while he searched their

surroundings for the masked man. He was gone, along with the journal.

He turned back to Liliana, surprised that she'd had the wherewithal to save him.

Tears slowly formed in her eyes. The sleeve of her dress was torn, but she appeared otherwise unharmed. "Why did they attack us?" she croaked.

He shook his head. "It was a distraction," he explained.

The thugs had attacked so that the masked man might escape. Arhyen had nothing else of value that random street hooligans would want to steal. The moment he pulled a dagger, they should have surveyed the risk and ran.

His gaze moved to the man who'd caught said dagger. A growing pool of blood was forming beneath him, weaving its way between the cobblestones of the street. This was *not* good. If someone had heard Liliana scream, officers of the Watch might be on their way at that very moment.

He approached the man and pulled his dagger out of his back, taking just a moment to wipe the extra blood on the man's coat. He returned the dagger to its sheath within his coat, then grabbed Liliana's hand. "We need to get out of here," he instructed.

She nodded a little too quickly, her eyes wide with panic.

Arhyen tugged on her hand, coaxing her into a run, wincing as her boots clattered loudly on the cobblestones. They made their way down several twists and turns of various alleyways unmolested, with only the rats to witness their passing. Once they'd gained some distance from the scene of the crime, Arhyen slowed and let his breathing catch up with him. Doing his best to act natural, he pulled Liliana out on the main street, instantly blending in with the bustling crowd.

He kept her close, partially to keep track of her, and

partially to hide her torn sleeve. He didn't want any overly-ambitious young men deciding that she'd been abused and needed rescuing.

Neither spoke as they made their way through the throng. He considered not going straight to his home, for fear of being followed, but no one had any reason to follow him. They'd already stolen the journal.

With a dejected sigh, he turned down the street that would lead to his current home. Not only had he lost the contract of a lifetime, but he now had a murder on his hands. He glanced at Liliana, walking by his side. He couldn't even begin to think about *that* complication. All he could really think in that moment, was that he needed a drink, and it wasn't even noon.

CHAPTER 4

The apartment they entered was not at all what Liliana had expected, simply judging by the exterior. First they'd traveled through an area of town strewn with refuse, with many sinister looking individuals hanging about. Arhyen had advised her to keep to the shadows, and he'd done the same. Then they'd reached the door, which had been practically hidden in a narrow alleyway, within a nook between two buildings. Few would happen upon the door by accident.

It made Liliana nervous that Arhyen felt the need to live in a well hidden place, but she supposed she couldn't really judge him. She'd come from a secret compound far out in the countryside, after all.

After unlocking a series of locks with multiple keys spread about his person, Arhyen had held open the door, waiting for her to go inside. Before she'd taken more than two steps, he'd instructed her to avoid a nearly invisible, ankle-height wire spanning the length of the entryway, far enough into the room to not be hit by the door when it opened.

As Arhyen shut and locked the door, Liliana walked further into the apartment, casually attempting to investigate. Her father had taught her that it was rude to look through other people's belongings, but she'd been around only her father's belongings for so long, she found the need to look about almost irresistible. She approached one of the tall book cases that lined the walls, filled to bursting with a mix of leather-bound tomes and cheaper covers that looked like some sort of paper. She resisted the urge to snatch one of the books from the shelves. Her father had *many* books, but she'd read them all too many times to count.

She glanced over her shoulder to see Arhyen watching her from near the doorway, then quickly looked away. Her eyes did a quick scan of the rest of the apartment. The space was small, but well organized. A bed was pushed against the far wall, while the center of the room was dominated by a large sofa, stuffing emerging in places through the dark blue fabric. A low table, covered with neat stacks of paper, stood in front of the sofa. The corner directly to the right of the door boasted a sink, stove, and a short countertop. In the opposite corner of the room, directly ahead of where Liliana stood, was a single door, presumably the bathroom, since she did not see one elsewhere.

She was only really accustomed to the facilities of her home, but had read descriptions of other homes in books, and had even seen a few illustrations. Basing her deductions off her limited knowledge, she deemed Arhyen's home rather normal, except for the obscured doorway, and wire at the entrance.

He came to stand beside her, a wry look on his face, but he didn't call her rude for observing everything. In fact, he seemed to be amused by her actions. "I was going to have you wait here while I delivered your father's journal," he explained, "but I suppose that's no longer a valid plan, since I no longer have it."

Picking up on the bitterness in his tone, Liliana realized something with a start. He'd only taken her along because she'd shown him where the journal was. Now that the journal had been stolen, did that invalidate their deal? He'd still taken her to his apartment, but would he soon force her to leave, seeing no further value in her?

"Your father didn't keep copies of that journal, did he?" he added hopefully, interrupting her thoughts.

Feeling deflated, she shook her head and used her long, red hair to obscure her face. "Most of his work resided within his memory. He kept only a single copy of each new formula, just in case."

He moved past her and slumped down on the sofa, then turned his head to regard her. She had the urge to step forward and rearrange his messy hair. Her father's hair had always been perfectly groomed. "And what about *your* memory?" he questioned.

Something akin to hope blossomed inside her. She *had* transcribed most of her father's notes herself . . . though there had been many, and it was difficult to keep them all straight. Still, she'd paid special attention to the formulae in the now missing journal, wondering at what they were truly meant to create. Her father had claimed that he'd used them to manufacture her soul. She clutched her chest as she thought about it. She liked the idea of having a soul, though she wasn't sure if one *really* resided inside her. She'd read through much of her father's literature, and had obtained the information that the creation of a soul was impossible. Not only was it impossible, the very idea was *evil*. Perhaps it was better if she didn't share that information?

"Well?" Arhyen pressed.

She sighed and once again glanced around the apartment. Grand it was not, but it was better than being alone in the dark. "I could probably remember," she began, "given the time. It would help if I had reference material to look over. Sometimes I forget the symbols."

Arhyen leapt to his feet. Before she knew it, he'd put his hands on her waist, and lifted her from the ground as he spun in place. As soon as he put her down she stumbled with dizziness, but he effortlessly caught her with a hand at her back. "How utterly brilliant!" he exclaimed happily.

She stared up at him, confused, and still a little dizzy.

He frowned, then laughed as he pushed his shaggy hair out of his face. Seeming to realize their closeness, he stepped away from her. "Sorry for the sudden excitement. I was simply overcome with joy that I brought you to London."

She smiled as something like elation filled her heart.

"Who knew that you'd make such an excellent back up plan?" he added.

Her heart dropped. For a moment there, she thought he actually *wanted* her along, when really, he was just using her for information. It didn't matter. With sudden resolve, she straightened her spine and lifted her nose in the air. She was using him so she could find her purpose in life, after all. It was no different.

"What do we do next?" she asked blandly.

Arhyen seemed to lose some of his joy, but explained, "I suppose first I'll acquire the reference books you mentioned. I'll need to stall my employer. I'd rather not let him know the journal was stolen. I'll of course supply you with anything else you may need. You're doing me a *huge* favor."

Liliana nodded and internally reassured herself, *If he was going to use her, she would use him too.* "*Anything* I need?" she pressed.

He suddenly seemed a bit nervous, but nodded. "Yes, anything, unless it's something absurd like asking me to assassinate the queen."

She inhaled sharply. She didn't know what he was talking about, but it didn't matter, as long as he could help her. "In exchange for recreating my father's journal, I need you to find my purpose," she stated bravely.

Arhyen leaned further away from her in surprise. "Your purpose?"

She nodded. "Everyone needs a purpose. Your purpose it to steal journals for people. That cafe man's purpose is to bring people tea and sweets. I need a purpose."

Arhyen's lips formed an *oh* of understanding. "You mean you want an *occupation.*"

She pursed her lips in thought. "Is stealing journals an occupation?"

Arhyen laughed. "Not in and of itself, but it is *part* of an occupation."

Liliana's mechanical heart sped as she had as sudden idea. "Can you teach *me* how to steal journals?"

Arhyen frowned, then patted her shoulder. "I'm not sure you know what you're asking."

She pouted. She was so sure she'd had a very good idea. "What is your occupation called?" she asked, hoping to clarify what she wanted from him.

He chuckled. "Most would call me a thief, though I do other things too."

She nodded in acceptance. "That settles it. My condition for recreating what was in father's journal, is that you must teach me to become a thief."

Arhyen balked, which made Liliana feel all the more satisfied with how she'd taken control of the situation. If being a thief was Arhyen's purpose, then perhaps it could be her purpose too.

Arhyen's eyes seemed to be slightly bulging out of his head, but finally, he nodded. "If that's truly your desire, I suppose I'm not in a position to say no."

Despite his obvious reservations, Liliana's spirits lifted. "When do we start?" she asked happily.

He tsked at her. "The first rule as my new pupil is that you must have patience. Right now, I must meet with my employer to buy us some time, and I'll try to find you some reference books on the way back. Then tonight, your training will begin."

Liliana couldn't contain her excitement. She wanted to remain poised, but knew it shined through in her stance and expression. "What will my first night of training entail?" she couldn't help but ask.

He winked at her. "We're going to find out who stole your father's journal, and *why*."

She frowned. "But we won't need it if I can recreate it . . . " she trailed off.

He answered with a curt nod. "Be that as it may, as the greatest thief in all of London, I cannot let the perpetrator go unpunished. I've never failed a job, and I don't intend to start now."

She nodded in acceptance. As long as she was still needed, she wanted to find out why someone had stolen the journal from them too. "But how will we find anything out? The man who took the journal wore a mask."

Arhyen grinned, then began to pace around the apartment. "Remember how I mentioned that stealing journals, and other things, for that matter, is only part of what I do?" He moved to a shelf and started pulling items out of his coat pockets, only to replace them with new items.

Following him across the room, she nodded.

"The other thing I'm good at is finding information," he continued, moving to another shelf to retrieve a notebook. "You'll have to learn both traits if you expect to become a successful thief."

Excitement filled her once again. "I'll work hard to recreate the journal, and I'll learn everything you have to teach me," she assured.

He smiled and held out his free hand to her. She was familiar with the gesture, but had never actually participated. She reached out hesitantly, and his large palm encased her gloved hand and gave it a hearty shake.

Their hands parted, and Arhyen strode across the room to where he'd left his satchel. Lifting it in his grasp, he placed the notebook inside, then moved to paw through a kitchen drawer with his free hand. "I shouldn't be gone long," he explained as he next moved to the bookcase, removed a book, placed a few sheets of paper inside of it from within his satchel, then replaced it. "Just an hour or two to meet with my employer, then another hour to gather your books," he continued.

Liliana watched him curiously, resisting the urge to examine his discarded items.

Satchel slung across his shoulder, he walked back to the designated kitchen area and began cutting slices from a large loaf of bread. As he proceeded to make himself a sandwich, he continued. "No one is likely to bother you here, but I'd appreciate it if you remained inside with the door locked." He paused his activities to look over his shoulder and meet her eyes. "Don't open the door for *anyone*, even if they knock politely. Whoever it is will come back if they have business with me." He turned back to his sandwich preparations.

She was beginning to feel nervous about being left alone in the apartment. Sure, there were locks on the door, and she was quite accustomed to being alone, but she knew nothing of the city. What if something caught fire, and she had to evacuate? What if one of the officers they'd seen at the gate came calling? Was she to ignore his knocks as well? She slumped down onto the nearby sofa, feeling dizzy.

She heard crinkling, and turned to watch as Arhyen wrapped his sandwich in a piece of parchment. He stuffed the wrapped sandwich into his satchel, then turned to look at her. Seeing her expression, his face grew concerned. "Are you well?"

She nodded, but it made her even more dizzy. Everything was happening so quickly. She'd only just gotten to London, and now she was already going to be left on her own.

He frowned, but took her word for it. "Remember what I told you," he ordered. "Just stay here, and I'll be back soon."

She nodded again, and a moment later he was out the door. She heard the sound of several locks being turned, then the sound of his footsteps as they echoed down the street. She remained on the sofa and looked down at her hands in her lap. He hadn't told her what she was supposed to *do*. Whenever her father had failed to give her direction, it meant she was supposed to remain by his side silently until he came up with a task for her. When her father would leave the compound, she was to sit in the study and wait for his return. Of course, she rarely obeyed on the latter. When her father was gone she would read his books, make up games to play with herself, and sometimes even experiment with minor alchemy, taking care to clean up her messes long before he returned.

She supposed she should apply the same tactics to the current situation. She was alone, after all. No one would know if she read the books, or did cartwheels across the apartment even. She laughed at her own thoughts. The books would do, and maybe a quick peek at the things Arhyen had removed from his pockets.

※

ARHYEN HURRIED DOWN THE STREET, WANTING TO accomplish his tasks as quickly as possible. He wasn't sure what had him so riled, but he felt uneasy leaving Liliana alone. No one was likely to bother her, but still, they'd left a body in an alleyway, and the masked man weighed heavy in his thoughts. Why had he stolen the journal? Could he have known what it contained? Few knew *why* Arhyen had ventured to the hidden compound, or that he had gone at all, but the information could have been obtained by any number of individuals. His best lead in that direction was his employer. It would be helpful to know if he'd told anyone else what he'd hired Arhyen for, but Arhyen didn't see an easy way to gather that information without admitting the journal had been stolen. He needed to avoid *that* at all possible costs.

Before he knew it, he was out of the slums and back onto one of the busy main streets. The citizens of London strolled about lazily, glancing in shops and ignoring the street hawkers pushing the sale of their goods. He trotted down the sidewalk toward his destination, plagued by his thoughts. If his employer gleaned that he had lost the journal, things wouldn't end well for him. This was a job he simply could not fail. He would have to think of an excuse to buy himself some time until Liliana could complete the formulae. *If* she could complete the formulae. In the mean time, they'd find out information on the masked man. He knew a few places to start, but unfortunately, that would position him to owe a few favors in the process.

He hurried through the market district until the crowds thinned and he was left looking at bleak office buildings filled with lawyers, accountants, and the like. All upstanding professions he'd never had the slightest bit of interest in. Thief might not be a respectable vocation, but at least it wasn't *boring*. He frowned as his thoughts turned back to Liliana, and the absurd notion of her becoming a thief. He doubted she knew what she was asking, but did it matter? *Probably*. He'd continually repeated to himself that she wasn't a real person, but then why did she have wants and desires just like any normal human? Why would she care about her purpose, if she didn't have real emotions? Why would she care about anything?

The answers to all his questions eluded him. Perhaps she really did have a soul. He was no alchemist, so who was he to say what was or wasn't possible?

He took a deep breath as he left the rows of office buildings behind to enter a wealthy residential district. *The* wealthy residential district. The rows of mansions were referred to by most as *White Heights*, though the name wasn't official. Anyone who was anyone lived along the well-maintained cobblestone streets, all bordered by tall, ornate iron fences, painted a uniform white to match the mansions they guarded.

Arhyen paused as he reached his destination and straightened his tan coat, its pockets filled with knives and other means of distraction should he need to escape danger. He looked up at the imposing white gates and the green grass beyond them. Though he was dressed to fit in with the wealthier class, even out on the street he felt out of place. No matter how much time he spent among the upper classes, he always felt like a fraud.

His stomach growled as he considered his options. He only then remembered his sandwich, but it was too late to eat it now. He wasn't about to enter the imposing mansion with condiments and bread crumbs smeared across his face.

With a hiss of steam, the gate swung inward, seemingly of its own volition. Someone had obviously spotted him from within the mansion, and had pulled the lever to open the steam-powered gates. Forgetting about his sandwich, Arhyen began his journey up the long, white gravel driveway, bordered by perfectly manicured green grass. In front of the mansion he could see a shiny black automotive, a new invention, limited strictly to the wealthy. Automotives were coal-powered, the same concept as trains, though they didn't require rails to guide them. He'd never ridden in one, and probably never would.

His heart was racing by the time he reached the end of the long driveway, to stand beside the automotive and the mansion's ornate double doors. He'd taken a few steps toward the gleaming wood of the door, when it swung inward, revealing a female automaton in traditional black and white maid's garb. The girl seemed nothing like Liliana, staring at him with entirely blank eyes beneath her blonde bangs. Her face was so lifeless, it could have been made of porcelain. She stood aside and gestured silently for him to enter.

He did as he was bade. His silent boots padded across the gold-flecked marble floor until he reached the middle of the grand entry room. An ornate staircase, almost as wide as his entire apartment, loomed before him.

The man he'd come to meet glided down the stairs in his ivory suit, sliding a hand down the narrow lapels of his short jacket. His blue eyes sparkled behind thin-rimmed, gold spectacles. His cream-colored loafers, likely more expensive than the automotive outside, squeaked on the immaculate tile floor as he came to stand before Arhyen. His name was Clayton Blackwood, and he was one of the most powerful men in London. He was born into nobility, but that had little to do with the power he held. He was an investor of sorts, and scoured the world over for new inventions to fund. Unfortunately, the actual inventors often ended up losing out on the deal. Sometimes they even lost their lives. As if the money of new inventions wasn't already enough, he also owned several steel mills, and had stock in the railroads.

"Did you find it?" Clayton asked, smoothing back his short, golden hair with a smooth flick of his wrist. He'd likely rehearsed the movement countless times in the mirror.

"I found many things," Arhyen answered with a sly grin, feigning confidence. "It may take me a few days to sort through them, but once I find a match for the sample you provided, I'll bring it straight here. I simply came to report that my venture to the hidden compound was a success."

Clayton frowned, instantly crumpling his facade of good cheer. "Bring all of the materials to me," he demanded. "I will sort them myself."

Arhyen did his best to keep his breathing even. "If that is your wish . . . " he trailed off. "I don't mind skipping the task of sorting through countless journals, covered in dust, mold, and other unmentionables. Why, I'm sure my hands would be black with filth by the time I finished."

At the small, nervous twitch of Clayton's immaculately groomed hands, Arhyen knew he had him. Clayton Blackwood was terrified of all forms of filth, which was ironic considering his hands were metaphorically more dirty than any of the vagrants the man so utterly detested.

"Fine," Clayton snapped. "But be quick about it."

Arhyen nodded, glad he'd decided against questioning his employer on whom he might have told about the journal.

Clayton waved a hand carelessly at the automaton. "See Monsieur Croft to the door," he ordered, though the door was only about two yards away. With that, he turned and glided back up the stairs, pausing on the fourth or fifth step to look over his should at Arhyen.

"And Arhyen?" he said softly.

Arhyen looked up at him.

"You know what happens when my employees fail," he muttered ominously.

Arhyen replied with a bow of his head. Yes, he knew exactly what happened when employees of Clayton Blackwood failed. They became one with the dirt their employer so utterly despised.

As the automaton maid saw him out, he thought once again of Liliana. If he was unable to recover the original journal, his life would quite literally depend on her. He hoped she'd been made with an excellent memory. If not, his illustrious thieving career might soon come to a grisly end.

CHAPTER 5

L iliana sat on the couch, glancing anxiously back at
the loaf of bread on the counter. Would it be rude
for her to try a bite? The chocolate cake she'd had
earlier had been divine, and she couldn't help but wonder
what other tastes were out there for her to try. She'd looked
through Arhyen's books, and found many she hoped to
read, but had resisted, fearing she'd be caught in the
process. She'd also found many items around the apartment
that she'd never seen before, and desperately wanted to
inquire about their function, especially the items that had
been removed from his pockets. Some she recognized as
weapons, but others, tiny glass capsules filled with various
shades of liquid, she'd never seen before.

A knock on the door interrupted her thoughts. She
froze, unsure of what to do. Arhyen had instructed her not
to open the door for *anyone*. She waited for several heartbeats, then the knock sounded again. She stared at the
closed door. The knock sounded a third time.

"Time to pay up!" a voice shouted from outside.

She jumped at the sudden shout, then let out a long

49

breath. She recognized that voice. It was Arhyen's associate from the previous night, the one who'd gained them access to the city. Arhyen had said not to open the door for anyone, but did this man count? He'd helped them back at the gates. What if he could help them some more? He'd known those who guarded the city gates, so did that mean he was a detective or officer of some sort? Would not answering the door make her a lawbreaker?

The man grumbled something under his breath. She could tell he was about to leave. Not taking the time to consider her actions any further, she leapt from the couch and raced toward the door, careful to hop over the ankle-height wire still strung tight near the threshold.

She fumbled with the various locks until the door swung inward.

Ephraim stared down at her in surprise, his black fedora shielding his eyes from the sun. "He's got you answering doors now, has he?" he asked.

She blinked up at him nervously. "Actually, he told me *not* to answer the door."

He raised a pale eyebrow at her. "Then why did you?"

"I just thought–" she stifled her words, realizing that she'd opened the door because she *hadn't* really thought. Or she had, but she'd simply come to the wrong conclusion.

His amused smile did nothing to soothe her embarrassment. "I take it Arhyen is not in?" he inquired, his eyes flicking to her torn sleeve, then back to her face.

She shook her head, tossing her long hair around her shoulders and nervously covering her sleeve with her hand. "He should be back soon."

Ephraim leaned forward, making Liliana suddenly nervous. "A word of advice," he whispered. "Next time you *don't* answer the door. You should also not tell any visitors where Master Croft is, nor when he shall return."

"Sound advice," a voice said from outside.

Arhyen appeared in the doorway behind Ephraim, holding shopping bags in each hand and wearing a tired expression on his face.

Ephraim laughed as he turned to Arhyen. "I imagine you know why I'm here?"

Arhyen nodded, then stepped around Ephraim and through the doorway as Liliana moved aside. "Do come in," he said somewhat snidely.

Ephraim followed Arhyen inside, stepping over the wire, just as Arhyen had, without missing a beat. Liliana suspected Ephraim of venturing into Arhyen's apartment many times before. Her suspicions were somewhat confirmed when he immediately made himself comfortable on the sofa, while Arhyen dropped his shopping bags on the floor near the stove, then moved to shut and lock the door.

Arhyen's eyes met Liliana's as she stood near the kitchen area, unsure of what to do.

He smiled at her, though she thought it seemed rather bedraggled. "Would you mind making some tea?" he asked hopefully.

She nodded quickly, gladly accepting the task, then turned her attention to the small gas stove while Arhyen went to sit with Ephraim. There was already a kettle out on the burner, which she retrieved and filled with water from the nearby sink. After she set the water to boil, she peeked through the few cabinets for tea and cups, listening intently to the men's conversation.

At first, they seemed to just be catching up, talking about the weather and other boring things. Then Ephraim announced that it was *time to pay up*.

Liliana fumbled the tea cup in her hand, nearly dropping it to the floor, though neither of the men seemed to notice. She took a shaky breath and set the cup on the counter, forcing herself to keep her eyes forward, though she had the urge to peek at Arhyen's expression.

Arhyen laughed, and Liliana fumbled a second cup as she removed it from the cabinet. "You're in luck," he replied. "As of early this morning, the rumors I have to deliver became much more interesting. You'll get your payment and then some."

Liliana continued to listen as she finished preparing the tea. It was a soothing task for her, something she'd done for her father a thousand times over, but Arhyen's words weren't soothing in the least. She listened as he told Ephraim all about their masked attacker, though he didn't include the part about being distracted by the three thugs, and her father's journal. The only other things he left out were the formulae within the journal, and the fact that she was an automaton.

"I didn't think Fairfax Breckenridge had any family, let alone a daughter," she heard Ephraim say in disbelief.

"Well he does, or he *did*," Arhyen replied, "though I'd appreciate if you kept that information to yourself. I don't want anyone bothering the poor girl."

"Of course," Ephraim assured.

Liliana frowned at being called a *poor girl*, but plastered a smile on her face as she carried the kettle and two cups, all placed on a small tray, to the table in front of the couch.

Arhyen glanced down at the tray, then turned his attention to her. "Oh, I'm sorry, did I not have enough clean cups?" He began to stand. "Let me wash one."

She became flustered as she realized her mistake. She'd assumed that she wasn't allowed to have tea. Her father always drank his tea alone, or with visitors, but she was never invited.

"I-I," she stammered, not sure how to explain herself. If

he went to the cupboard he'd see that there were two more clean teacups, and she'd look a fool for not bringing a third.

Seeming to suddenly comprehend her situation, he waved her off. "I forgot, I'm trying to cut back," he lied. "Thank you for the reminder."

Ephraim raised an eyebrow at the exchange, but didn't comment. Instead, he poured tea into the two cups, and offered one to Liliana.

She took it appreciatively, then took Arhyen's seat on the couch as he stood and offered it to her. She gazed down into her cup, taking a deep breath to regain her composure. It was quite flustering to be treated like a human being.

"What do you intend to do while you're in London?" Ephraim asked.

It took Liliana a moment to realize he was speaking to her. She jumped, almost spilling her tea, then smiled apologetically. "Well," she began, "Arhyen is going to teach me to-"

"Cook!" Arhyen cut her off.

She glared at him for interrupting, but his worried gaze prompted her to keep quiet. Perhaps her mission to find her purpose was supposed to remain a secret.

Ephraim snickered, then glanced up at Arhyen. "You cook?"

Arhyen bristled and stood a little straighter. "Quite well, actually."

Ephraim didn't seem to believe him, but he let it go. He placed his full tea cup on the table, then cleared his throat. "I really should be going, but since you've given me a great deal of information, I'll offer you something in return." He stood. "You are not the first victims of our mysterious masked man," he explained, "nor do I believe you'll be the last. He has robbed several wealthy estates that we know of, taking only one item at a time. In each case, those who witnessed the thefts claimed he simply disappeared, like a ghost."

"What has he stolen?" Arhyen asked curiously.

Ephraim shrugged. "Odds and ends, really. So far he's taken several old alchemical tomes, an antique dagger, and an urn."

"Was the urn-" Arhyen began.

"Filled with ashes, yes," Ephraim replied.

Arhyen nodded, seemingly deep in thought.

Liliana didn't think she fully understood the significance of the conversation, so she remained silent.

"Well, I'm off," Ephraim announced. He bowed slightly in front of her, then walked around the sofa toward the door before turning back to Arhyen. "Inform me if you come across anything pertinent?"

Arhyen nodded absentmindedly, then Ephraim let himself out of the apartment, minding the wire by the doorway.

Liliana turned to stare at Arhyen, hoping for an explanation.

He stood there thinking awhile longer, then nodded to himself. He glanced at her. "I apologize, but I should probably get some rest before tonight. We may be out quite late, and I must admit, I've reached the end of my reserves."

She nodded, feeling disappointed. If she was to discover her purpose, she needed all the information she could get, but she would not push him when he'd already done so much for her.

He gestured to his forgotten shopping bags, still resting near the stove. "There are your books, and a few other things I thought you might need. If any of it is not what you require, or not to your liking, feel free to speak up."

She glanced at the bags and felt suddenly less disappointed. He'd said books and other *things*. What might they contain? Suddenly she couldn't wait for him to go to sleep.

Arhyen turned away from her and stumbled over to the bed against the far wall. He tossed himself onto the mattress, face down and fully clothed, then seemed to fall asleep within seconds.

Liliana waited and sipped her rapidly cooling tea for several more minutes to ensure that Arhyen was asleep, then stood and hurried over to the bags. She knelt on the wooden floor and set down her teacup, then pulled the nearest bag toward her. This one was all books, ranging from the fundamentals of alchemy all the way to advanced formulae. Her father had possessed many of the advanced books, though all would be useful when it came time to remember the specific symbols and formulae she needed. She really should have started on it right then, but she couldn't resist the temptation to see what was in the other bag.

Pushing the books aside, she curiously pulled it toward her. The first thing she pulled out was a fresh, leather-bound journal. She leafed through its blank pages, then set it aside. Next came a box that was lighter than she expected. She opened it to find soft, forest green fabric. She stood as she pulled the garment out of the box to reveal a new dress. The style was similar to the one she wore, with a fitted bodice, long sleeves, and skirts that flared away from the body for ease of movement, though the fabric was thicker, and more finely made. Still standing, she held the dress against herself, quite pleased. Draping the dress over her arm, she knelt near the bag once more, and found new underpinnings and stockings. Feeling embarrassed and not knowing why, she gathered all of the garments into her arms.

She glanced at Arhyen, lying face down on his pillow,

clearly still asleep, then hurried to the bathroom to change. She'd explored the small space earlier, and had deemed it the only appropriate place to change. Once inside, she shut the door and undid the numerous buttons going down her back, having to bend her arms awkwardly at times to reach them all. She removed her old underpinnings and donned the new ones, pleased to see that everything fit properly. She thought of Arhyen picking the items out, and felt suddenly dizzy and short of breath.

She shook her head and took a moment to calm herself, then slid into the dress. It fit perfectly, but she found that undoing the buttons on her old dress had been far more simple than buttoning the ones that went all the way up the back of her new dress. Growing increasingly flustered, she buttoned as many as she could, then looked at herself in the small, oval mirror mounted on the wall above the small sink.

The dress suited her coloring, she supposed. It made her skin look pale, while her hair seemed a more vibrant shade of red. Her large blue eyes shone in contrast. She took a moment to comb her fingers through her hair, but she'd lost all of the pins that had previously held it, so there was little else she could do to make herself presentable.

Feeling giddy in her new attire, and still slightly embarrassed about the underpinnings, she gathered her old clothing and exited the bathroom. She glanced at Arhyen, who was still asleep, his face buried in his pillow. Stepping lightly, she walked past the sofa and put her old clothes in the bag that had contained her new ones, then gathered up several of the books he'd purchased. She carried the books to the table in front of the sofa and spread them out across its surface before sitting. She glanced at Arhyen again, then retrieved the nearest book and started reading.

A few times as she read, he mumbled unintelligible

things in his sleep, making her smile. She found herself quite determined to live up to her end of their bargain, no matter what it might take.

⚜

ARHYEN SLOWLY ROLLED OVER, STRETCHING HIS ARMS above his head as he woke. The last rays of sunlight peeked weakly through the window. Why was he in bed at this hour?

He sat up bolt straight as things finally caught up to him. He turned to look at the sofa, then exhaled a sigh of relief to see Liliana sitting there happily in her new dress, sipping tea and perusing the books he'd gotten her. Her hair looked a little neater, and she seemed almost like a real human as her gaze turned to him.

"How long was I asleep?" he asked groggily.

"Several hours," she answered, then frowned as she lowered her tea to her lap. "Is that bad? Was I supposed to wake you? Father would sometimes sleep during the day, but it was rarely more than an hour."

Arhyen shook his head and lowered his feet to the wooden floor, then frowned as he realized he still wore his shoes. He hadn't perceived just how exhausted he'd been until his head had hit the pillow.

Liliana scrambled to stand up, pushing the books aside and hastily setting her teacup on the table. "T-thank you for the dress," she stammered.

Why was she so nervous? He thought back to the automaton at Blackwood's estate with her blank stare. Automatons weren't supposed to get nervous. He stood and took a few steps toward her, then looked her up and down. Her hair, which hung nearly to her waist, seemed brighter against the deep green fabric. "Well the aim was to blend in," he explained, "though I don't know that this dress will accomplish that task for you."

She blinked up at him. "W-what?"

He shook his head, not about to explain to her what he meant. "You look lovely," he corrected.

She looked down at her feet, seemingly embarrassed. What had he gotten himself into?

"Um," she began, then cut herself off, twisting her lips as if debating her next words.

"Yes?" he pressed.

Instead of speaking, she quickly turned around, putting her back to him, revealing that the portion of her dress between her shoulder blades had not been buttoned.

"Ah," he observed, realizing her quandary. He gently began to fasten the rest of the buttons, taking care to touch her as little as possible, since she seemed so apprehensive about it.

"There you go," he stated once he was done, then moved past her toward the kitchen, effectively ending the awkward moment. As he started to slice some bread, he looked over his shoulder at her. She had turned around, her eyes fixed upon him. "Would you like a sandwich?" he asked.

At the question, he could almost swear he saw her mouth watering.

She nodded excitedly, then asked, "Is it normal to eat so many sandwiches?"

He shrugged, then turned back to his work. "It is for me."

Really, it was only his second sandwich of the day, and he'd only made one for the day before, which he'd thrown out since it had turned to mush in his satchel. It *was* his normal meal though. He'd lied when he told Ephraim that he could cook. He'd even burn plain rice if he tried to boil it.

He retrieved ham and some lettuce from the ice box, then finished assembling the other ingredients. Once they were complete, he set the sandwiches on plates to carry over to the sofa. Liliana took the plate he offered as she resumed her seat amongst her scattered books, then stared down at her meal like it was a work of art. He sat across from her, waiting patiently for her to take a bite.

"Go ahead," he urged, doing his best not to laugh at her.

Finally, she picked up the sandwich and took a bite, then her eyes lit up. She chewed quickly and swallowed. Within less than a minute, the sandwich was no more.

Arhyen shook his head and chuckled as he ate his own sandwich, thinking it was exceedingly cruel of her *father* to create a being with the propensity for taste, only to deny her something so simple as a sandwich, or a piece of chocolate cake.

She watched him as he continued to eat. Eventually he gave up and offered her the leftover half. She took it with a grin. He found that he quite liked seeing her smile, automaton or no.

CHAPTER 6

A s night fell, they prepared to leave Arhyen's small apartment. Liliana had never been more nervous in her life. Not only was she embarking on a new start, she would perhaps be uncovering more information about *what* she was. Why had the masked man stolen her father's journal, and why had someone hired Arhyen to steal it in the first place? She supposed she could just ask Arhyen about the latter, but she could admit, if only to herself, that she was frightened of the possible answer.

She had studied the books Arhyen provided for hours while he slept, and had begun to scribble notes in the fresh journal. She had actually remembered more than she thought she would. A few more hour's work, and perhaps she could get everything down correctly. Yet, she was hesitant to finish. She'd perused the formulae many times, knowing they were the ones that gave her a *soul*, as her father claimed, but the process didn't entirely make sense to her. For one thing, the page did not contain just one formula. There were *four*. Had four different components been required to give her a soul, or had she simply been given something else?

"Are you ready?" Arhyen asked from across the room.

She startled, unsure of how long she'd been standing near the sofa, entirely lost in thought. Her eyes met Arhyen's, then she looked him up and down. He'd changed into black wool trousers and a gray silk waistcoat over a high-collared, pinstriped shirt. Atop his messy brown hair rested a black bowler cap.

He pulled a pocket watch out of his waistcoat to check the time. "We should really get going," he prompted.

Liliana nodded quickly and strode forward to meet him near the door, but Arhyen hesitated before reaching for the knob. He held a finger up, gesturing for her to wait, then hurried back across the room, pausing by a pile of coats draped over a rickety chair near the bed. He pawed through the pile, coming away with a simple black coat. He returned to her and wrapped it around her shoulders.

"Sorry," he muttered, looking her up and down. "I should have thought to purchase you a proper coat."

She touched the new fabric at her shoulders. "I do not feel the cold as much as . . . others," she said awkwardly, not wanting to fully explain herself. She could tell when it was cold, but it wasn't terribly uncomfortable for her, nor would it cause her to fall ill.

He patted her shoulder absentmindedly and reached for the door. "Yes, but it will seem odd for a lady to be out on a chilly night without a coat."

Her mouth formed an *oh* of comprehension. They were trying to blend in.

Arhyen opened the door and she followed him outside. While he turned various keys in various locks, Liliana took in their surroundings, what she could see of them, anyway.

There was only a sliver of moon in the sky, and no street lamps in that area of town, leaving them in near darkness.

Arhyen remained by her side as they began to walk, occasionally herding her in one direction or another, any time they needed to turn down a different street. At first, Liliana worried about losing their way in the darkness. Everything in the area looked the same, even during the *day*. Without the sun, the bland buildings were entirely unremarkable. Yet, Arhyen seemed to know just where they were going, and soon they reached a more populated area lit with street lamps. He took her arm in his, presumably so she wouldn't get lost in the growing crowd of nighttime denizens, and Liliana began to relax. She breathed in the heady night air, tinged with a sweet, flowery scent wafting off many of the women they passed. Another scent, more pungent and acrid than the first, hit her nostrils any time they passed an open door.

Arhyen guided her along past many busy establishments filled with laughter and the smell of food. She looked at each one longingly, wishing to go inside. She wanted to be a part of that laugher, and she especially wanted to eat that food, but unfortunately, they kept walking.

Finally, just when she'd almost lost hope, Arhyen stopped in front of a wooden door. There were no windows on the face of the short, brick building, but she could hear conversation and laughter emanating from within. Arhyen knocked on the door, and a little metal hatch she'd failed to notice before slid open. A pair of eyes could be seen peering out at them, then the hatch slid shut, and the door opened.

Arhyen waited while Liliana went in ahead of him, then quickly followed after her. The noise within the place was louder than expected, almost as loud as the train they'd ridden the previous night. The clinking of glasses mingling with the raucous conversation made Liliana feel almost dizzy, and the sensation wasn't helped along by the thick, hazy air. She noticed several patrons holding cigarettes to their lips, and the acrid smell she'd noticed outside suddenly made sense. Her father had often smoked tobacco from a wooden pipe, but this smoke smelled slightly different, or perhaps she just wasn't used to such a large amount of it.

"This way," Arhyen whispered in her ear. He pulled the coat from her shoulders and hung it from a nearby rack.

The man guarding the door eyed Liliana curiously, probably because she'd been staring at the whole scene in awe. He was a full head taller than Arhyen, and twice as wide, with no hair on his lumpy scalp and several scars littering his face. Suddenly terrified that she'd drawn too much of the man's attention, she hurried ahead of Arhyen in the direction he'd pointed out to her.

Many of the male patrons looked her up and down as she passed, and quite a few of the women too. Some murmured their hellos to Arhyen, and a few inquired about his new *lady friend*. Joking with a few, but ignoring most, Arhyen placed his hand at the small of Liliana's back and hustled her through the crowd.

They reached the end of the room, and the long span of wooden bar, to find a curtained doorway. Not bothering to knock or announce himself, Arhyen pushed the curtain aside. Liliana walked through, as instructed, then he followed, allowing the curtain to fall shut behind him.

Inside was a small, dimly lit room with a single table in its center. The table was scattered with cards and poker chips, just like the ones her father had owned. Around the table sat four men and two women. All turned to gaze at them, though Liliana was more entranced by the poker set. She'd thought her father's had been special, but apparently it was not, as the black, red, and green chips looked exactly the same.

One of the men, with silver hair and a patch over his eye, waved to them in greeting. "I see you've brought something far more valuable to bet than coin, Arhyen," he observed.

Liliana wasn't quite sure what the man meant, but Arhyen seemed to take it in stride. "Just coin tonight, I'm afraid. This jewel I'm keeping for myself." He offered her a wink as everyone at the table shifted seats to make available two side by side.

Arhyen approached the table and held one chair out for Liliana, placing her next to one of the women, then took the other seat himself, next to a gangly man with a horribly prominent adam's apple, and a week's worth of stubble on his grimy chin.

The stranger seated on Liliana's left, a woman in her upper years with her hair done up in a prim, gray bun, wearing a black dress with a collar all the way up to her throat, gave Liliana a shrewd look with her hawk-like eyes, then turned her attention back toward the cards in her hands.

Liliana watched as Arhyen reached into his breast pocket and withdrew a wad of bills. He threw them in the center of the table, and eyepatch man pushed a stack of chips toward him.

"Your girl not playing?" eye patch man asked with a crooked grin.

"No," Arhyen began, but Liliana cleared her throat to interrupt him.

He turned to her, surprise clear in his light brown eyes.

"I know how to play," she said weakly, suddenly regretting drawing attention to herself.

Arhyen laughed and pushed half of his chips in front of her. "This I'd like to see."

Those already playing finished their hands, and the chips in the center were pushed toward the unfriendly woman on Liliana's left. The other woman at the table, many years younger than the first, with strongly rouged lips and dark hair, gathered the cards in her black-gloved hands, expertly shuffled them, then dealt everyone a new hand. Liliana lifted the cards placed in front of her, hoping these people played by the same rules her father had taught her.

The betting began, and she mimicked the others, unsure of how much each chip was worth. Next, cards were exchanged for new ones, more betting ensued, and it was time to show the hands of those remaining in the game, just Arhyen, the gangly man, and all three women, including Liliana. She observed each hand as they were placed upon the table, but was hesitant to act, as she was unsure if these people had different rules.

"You won," Arhyen commented, somewhat surprised, then laughed.

Eyepatch man pushed the chips in the center toward her, and another round took place. She did her best to keep from grinning. Her father had taught her that one shouldn't gloat when they won at something, but it was difficult to resist.

As the night wore on, she won several more rounds, and conversation began to pick up. Those around the table spoke of many things, but mainly rumors of occurrences within the city, as well as the business of other people not present.

"I have one," the gangly man announced, wanting to take a turn at divulging information. "I heard from me butcher that Fairfax Breckenridge has disappeared, and that all the alchemists in the city are after his research."

If Liliana's heart wasn't mechanical, it would have stopped. They were talking about her father. Arhyen cast her a wary glance, then turned to the gangly man. "What would they want with his notes?" he asked curiously. "Surely he researched nothing that the rest of them don't already know."

The gangly man shook his head in reply, but another man, one appearing around Arhyen's age, but wearing suspenders and a top hat, spoke up, "I heard he was researching dangerous compounds for warfare, like smoke bombs, but with a bit more punch."

Eyepatch man shook his head. "No, that's not right. I heard he was researching medicine."

The young woman with the rouged lips leaned forward conspiratorially. "You want to know what I heard?" she asked.

Everyone at the table, save Liliana and the older woman, nodded. "I heard that he was trying to create the essence of the human soul."

Liliana gasped. She had a dreadful, sick feeling in the pit of her stomach.

"I also heard he had a daughter," the woman added, "and the alchemists want to find her too, to see what she knows."

Liliana did her best to act naturally, but her hands trembled as she re-stacked the chips in front of her. The rouge-lipped woman watched her movements curiously. Liliana turned her gaze down toward the table, unsure of why the woman was watching her so intently.

Arhyen suddenly took her hand in his. "I think it's time to get my lady to bed," he announced lasciviously.

The men at the table erupted with laughter, but the rouge-lipped woman continued to watch Liliana. Arhyen helped her to stand, and she was overcome with gratitude, even if she was quite sure that he'd also made a joke at her expense. He could paint her up like a jester for all she cared, if it would get her out of that room.

Eye patch man exchanged their chips for bills, which Arhyen snatched up and stuffed in his pocket. The wad seemed to be thicker than what they'd started out with. He bowed toward the table. "Thanks for the game, gentlemen and ladies."

They all waved him off as they continued playing, and Arhyen guided Liliana toward the curtain. At the feeling of eyes on her back just before they exited, Liliana glanced over her shoulder to meet the dark gaze of the rouge-lipped woman. The woman offered her a knowing smile, then the curtain swung shut, barring her from Liliana's view.

"That was . . . interesting," Arhyen remarked as they left the room behind them.

"We went there for information," Liliana observed weakly.

Arhyen smirked, placing a hand at the small of her back to guide her forward. "Of course. There's no other reason to play cards with amateurs."

Liliana didn't think the people in the room had been amateurs in the slightest, but she didn't comment. The exterior room now had a more sleepy feel to it. The conversation was just a dull murmur, and the glasses on the tables were all empty. No one paid them any mind as they walked past.

They reached the door, still guarded by the massive man, and Arhyen retrieved the coat to drape back around her shoulders. The doorman stepped aside and allowed them to venture back out into the night. Liliana heaved a sigh of relief as the cool air hit her face.

"About what they said . . . " Arhyen trailed off, stopping about a yard away to stand in the halo of a street lamp.

Liliana shook her head, not wanting to discuss it. She took a step closer to him. "They know about me. So what?" she asked defensively.

He frowned. "You may be in danger."

She started walking, wanting to be as far away from the establishment as possible.

Arhyen had to jog to catch up with her. "I'll keep you safe," he assured, then paused. "Starting right now," he added.

At his words, Liliana glanced around them until her eyes landed on an alleyway across the street. A man in a cloak stood there. His smooth face reflected the moonlight. No, not his *face*. A mask.

As Liliana and Arhyen watched, the masked man lifted a black gloved hand and waved at them, then turned back down the alleyway and ran. Liliana moved to run after him, but Arhyen caught her arm. "This is clearly a trap," he growled under his breath.

"But we can't just let him get away," she countered.

Arhyen grunted in frustration, then let go of her arm. She was right. They jogged across the street side by side, then took off running down the alleyway where the man had disappeared.

❦

ARHYEN KNEW IT WAS A TERRIBLE IDEA TO CHASE AFTER the masked man, but Liliana had an excellent point. They *couldn't* just let him get away. Liliana's shorter legs were somehow carrying her faster that Arhyen's could carry him. He pushed himself harder, barreling down the dark alleyway, not wanting Liliana to run into danger ahead of him.

He rounded a corner and came to a sudden halt as Liliana stopped beside him. There was no sign of the masked man. Liliana looked to Arhyen, but something else has caught his eye. There in the moonlight, in the middle of the street, lay a single piece of paper with a rock holding it in place. The wind whipped at the paper's edges as the pair approached. Neither one speaking, Arhyen knelt to retrieve it.

He stood, his eyes skimming the words written on the parchment. Liliana peeked curiously over his shoulder. For her benefit, he began to read out loud, "My dearest daughter, if you're reading this, I have perished. There may be men looking for you, even now. As you know, my research was very important. It helped make you what you are. It is the reason I have been killed. You must take my journal, you know which one I mean, to a man named Victor Ashdown. He will care for you, just as I have. Liliana, there is one last thing you must remember. You are not human. You cannot live a normal life. Find Victor Ashdown, and he will explain everything."

Liliana looked up to Arhyen with wide eyes as he finished reading. "Why would this man have a note from my father?"

Arhyen stared down at the note with distaste. "There's no way for us to know that this note is actually from your father. This could simply be someone trying to trick us."

Liliana's eyes shimmered in the moonlight with unshed tears. "But what if it's real?"

"The first order of business is to find this Victor Ashdown. If we can locate him, then we'll have all of the information we need." He glanced around them as he spoke, but the masked man was gone. He shook his head. "Let's go home."

Liliana nodded somberly.

Feeling like he should say more, but not knowing if it would help, Arhyen led the way back to the street.

They walked together in silence for some time. A cool breeze picked up, making Arhyen glad Liliana still had his coat around her shoulders. He was just preparing to speak, when Liliana cleared her throat, and looked up at him. "How will we find this Victor Ashdown?"

"It shouldn't be too difficult," he assured her, glad she'd spoken first. "There are only so many people in the city, and Victor Ashdown is likely of some importance if your father would entrust him with such a task."

Liliana gazed up at the moon as they walked, not replying right away. He almost thought she wouldn't speak any further, when she said, "I cannot expect you to help me find him. I feel I've already asked far too much than our original bargain implied."

Arhyen almost laughed, the notion was so ridiculous. He was the one who had lost the journal. If he did not have Lilliana's memory to aid him, he would have been facing an inevitable death. Ignoring her statement, he replied, "We'll start asking around in the morning. I have some friends in the Postal Service that might have heard his name, but if not, there are many other ways to locate him. Your father expected you to find him on your own, so it shouldn't be a terribly difficult task."

Liliana fell silent. Her boots were the only sounds as they left the busy district of town. Though it was dark, Arhyen easily navigated the narrow streets that would lead them to his home. He walked cautiously, at any moment expecting another surprise visit from the masked man. He thought of the note now in his pocket, then shook his head. The masked man had already done his job. They would not see him again that night. Yet, if he had been previously hired by Liliana's father to deliver a message, then why had he stolen the journal? Perhaps the note was a fake, and the masked man wanted to lead them to Victor

Ashdown for some other reason. Arhyen had no idea what that reason might be. Perhaps Victor Ashdown could tell them.

He glanced at Liliana's face, illuminated by the soft moonlight. She deserved answers, and he was going to find them for her.

CHAPTER 7

Arhyen unlocked the numerous locks to the front door, then held it open and waited for Liliana to step inside, once again reminding her of the trip-wire. He felt bone tired, despite the long nap he'd taken. As he ventured inside the dark apartment and resealed the door, he realized yet another problem. Liliana stood near the sofa awkwardly. Did she sleep? He felt oddly uncomfortable at the thought of her remaining awake while he slept, even though that had been the situation earlier.

"You can take the bed," he offered, not wanting to put her on the spot by asking if she needed sleep.

Neither of them had bothered with turning on the lights, but in the dim light shining through the curtained window, he thought he saw a tear run down her face. She hovered near the sofa and her piles of alchemy books, pawing nervously at her hair

He moved toward her, then lifted his hands to comfort her, but hesitated, leaving them hanging in the air, unsure if it was alright to touch her. She looked up at him, allowing the moonlight to briefly illuminate her face, and the tears that rolled down her cheeks.

With a sigh of resignation, he lifted a hand to her cheek and wiped away the moisture.

She stared at him with wide eyes, seemingly startled by his decision to touch her.

"You should get some rest," he muttered.

She shook her head. "I don't sleep."

He glanced at the bed, then back to her. "You could try?"

She seemed to think for a moment, then nodded as more tears fell down her face. He gently guided her toward the bed and pulled back the heavy quilt. She sat stiffly, then slowly laid down, still fully dressed. Feeling a bit like he was taking care of a child, he moved to her feet and started unlacing her boots. He slipped off one boot, then the other, letting her feet fall back to the bed in turn while she stared up at the ceiling.

He placed her boots on the floor, then pulled the blankets over her. Satisfied that she was as comfortable as he could make her, he turned to move toward the sofa, but her voice stopped him.

"I've never laid in a bed before," she said quietly.

He glanced over his shoulder at her in the darkness. "My Lady, you haven't done many things before. It doesn't mean you shouldn't try them."

She laughed quietly. "So how does one sleep?"

He moved back to the bed and sat near her feet. "First, you close your eyes," he instructed. He waited for her to close her eyes, then continued, "Then you take deep, even breaths."

Her breathing slowed.

"Now you think about something pleasant," he continued softly.

"Like what?" she murmured.

He laughed quietly. "Like chocolate cake."

The moonlight illuminated her small smile and closed eyes.

"Just keep thinking about it," he whispered. He stood and slowly began to back away from the bed. "Then let your mind wander where it may." Reaching the sofa, he lowered himself to the cushions. "And try not to snore," he added quietly.

A soft chuckle emanated from the bed. Arhyen smiled, then listened for a while, until her breathing caught the gentle rhythms of sleep. He had not been sure that it would work, but he hoped she truly slept. He shut his eyes, and soon followed behind her.

ॐ

LILIANA AWOKE TO THE SMELL OF SOMETHING BURNING. She sat up in bed, more surprised by the feeling of waking up, than by the acrid scent of smoke. Though the smoke still held her concern. She glanced over her shoulder toward the kitchen to see Arhyen standing in front of the stove, softly cursing to himself as he scraped a spatula against a frying pan.

She rose from the bed and padded her stocking-clad feet across the floor to stand at his side. He glanced at her, then jumped in surprise, apparently not having heard her approach. She looked down at the blackened frying pan and the indiscernible charred mass contained within.

He cringed, then set down the spatula on the counter-top. His dark hair was a mess, sticking to his face with sweat at his temples. "How about we go out for breakfast?" he offered.

"I was hoping to work on the journal," she explained.

Not only did she suspect that Arhyen really needed it, but she was hoping someone would be able to tell them what the formulae inside would produce. Would it really create a soul, or was it something more nefarious? Part of her still hesitated to find out, but she knew that she must if she truly wanted to move on with her life.

"Honestly, I was hoping you would offer," he admitted. "I'm in a bit of a bind with my employer. He's not a terribly nice man."

Liliana nodded, then shooed Arhyen aside. She picked up the spatula and began scraping the remaining char from the pan, then glanced over to find him still watching her. Feeling uncomfortable, she emptied the pan into the waste bin, then wiped it clean with a nearby rag, already covered in a bit of char.

"I was hoping to make you breakfast, as a small apology for all I put you through," he explained. He moved to hover over her shoulder as she returned the pan to the stove.

She glanced back at him in surprise. "For all *you've* put *me* through?" she asked, astonished. "You wouldn't be involved in any of this if I hadn't insisted on following you when you came for father's journal."

"Ah, but I was the one who came for the journal in the first place," he countered, raising a finger in the air to emphasize his point.

Liliana sniffed petulantly, then dropped some oil into the pan and lit the burner. "And if you hadn't come for it. I would still be sitting there in the dark."

Arhyen shook his head and laughed as Liliana perused the ingredients on the countertop. There were few.

"We're equal partners then," he decided finally.

Liliana smiled as she looked down at the pan, liking the idea of having a partner, then the words from her father's letter echoed through her head, *You are not human. You cannot live a normal life.* Feeling suddenly melancholy, she reached for fresh eggs from a bowl on the countertop.

"So you can cook?" Arhyen questioned, still standing behind her as she began to crack the eggs into the pan.

"I cooked all my father's meals," she explained, feeling her voice hitch on the word *father*. Why had he made her if she was unable to lead a normal life? Had her purpose merely been to cook and clean, and to transcribe his notes?

She'd occasionally been allowed to meet a few of her father's colleagues, but they always looked upon her as a great invention, not a person. Had her father shared those views? He'd told her many times that he loved her, but perhaps it was not in the way that a father should love a daughter. Perhaps it was in the way that a carpenter might love a table carved by his own hands.

Arhyen watched her silently for a few minutes as she cooked the eggs, then moved to cut several slices of bread. "Perhaps if you take the morning to work on the journal," he began, "then I can begin the search for Victor Ashdown."

"I can't ask you to go to all that trouble yourself," she countered instantly, unwilling to state the true reason why she might want to delay that meeting. Her father's note had implied that Victor Ashdown was to take *possession* of her, and she wanted nothing to do with this unknown man. She was quite happy where she was, even though she worried about being a burden.

"You're putting all of this work into the journal for me," he explained, interrupting her thoughts. "The least I can do is begin the search, then you can join me this afternoon."

Arhyen placed the sliced bread on a plate with a side of butter while she finished the eggs, then divided them between two more plates. Once she had removed the pan from the stove, placing it upon a metal trivet on the countertop, Arhyen filled the teakettle with water and set it to boil. Soon the tea was ready, and together they carried the filled cups and food laden plates to the table in front of the sofa. She had at first thought it odd that Arhyen didn't have a dining room table. Her father always took his meals at a special table just for that purpose, but she found she enjoyed sitting at the sofa, instead of a more formal arrangement.

Seated on opposite ends of the sofa, they began to eat. She wasn't sure she liked eggs as much as she'd hoped. They had an odd, almost slimy texture that was unappealing, or perhaps it was just her cooking. Had she been making her father's eggs incorrectly all of those years? She reached for a slice of bread with butter, only to find that Arhyen had already eaten his half of bread, and had cleared his plate of eggs. How on earth had he eaten so fast? She suddenly began to grow nervous. If he was done eating, he would probably prepare to leave. She wasn't looking forward to being left alone in the apartment again, and the idea of finishing the journal only added to her anxiety.

Arhyen stood with his empty plate and took it into the kitchen, then returned to stand before her. "I won't be gone long," he explained, causing her stomach to drop. "We can go out for lunch and continue our search for information in the process. Hopefully by the time I return, I will already have some leads on Victor Ashdown."

Liliana nodded in acceptance, unwilling to reveal her petty fears. She wanted to ask him to stay, but could think of no adequate excuse. Resigned to her fate, she turned her attention to the alchemy books stacked on the table as Arhyen walked away and let himself out the front door. She heard the locks being slid into place from outside and couldn't help but twist her head to stare the door, hoping Arhyen would change his mind and return.

When locks stayed locked, and the closed door did not reopen, she turned back to her books, determined to focus on her task. She was quite sure she had learned all she could from their pages, and was now prepared to write the special formulae that Arhyen needed, though the books would still serve as a handy reference. She opened the blank journal, retrieved a pen from the table, and began to write.

Her hand slowly scrawled the components that had made her what she was. Would Victor Ashdown know what they meant? Would he tell her that she was just an object, like any other automaton? She felt a tear slip down her face as she considered the possible outcomes. If it turned out that she was just a soulless construct, she might as well just return to her home, to remain in darkness, never to emerge again.

⚘

Arhyen placed his bowler cap on his head as he strolled down the street. He would first pay a visit to one of his friends who worked for the Postal Service. The friend owed him numerous favors, and likely would not mind keeping an eye out for the name of Victor Ashdown to eliminate some of that debt.

Next, he would visit some of the local apothecaries to see if they had any valuable information. He would have to be cautious in his search to avoid drawing any unwanted attention. Word traveled fast throughout London, especially among the common folk, and he didn't want to alert Victor that someone was looking for him. Before that happened, he wanted ample time to scope Victor out. If Victor was a less than honorable character, then he would find a different way to discover the answers they sought. Liliana might not be his to protect, but he would not leave her in the hands of an indecent man.

Then, there was the fact that it was the masked man who had provided them with Liliana's father's letter. It could all be some elaborate trap, but to what end? He had already stolen Fairfax Breckenridge's journal. The only other thing he might want was Liliana herself. At that thought, he almost turned back around, but forced himself to move forward toward the busy London streets. If the masked man truly wanted her, he would have taken her the previous night, or when Arhyen left her alone in his apartment the previous day. It was something else. Something that had everything to do with Victor Ashdown.

Clouds moved to obscure the sun as he emerged onto the main street. It was often rainy in London, but for some reason, Arhyen felt the clouds held ill omens. He picked up his pace, barely even noticing his surroundings, so intent was he on his task. A few more blocks and he had reached the red brick walls of the postmaster's office. Hopefully William, known to his friends as Willy, would be inside. If not, Arhyen could not waste the time it would take to scour his route. Instead, he would continue on with his plans, then return for Willy later.

He was about to venture inside, when something caught his sight further up the street. It had only been the briefest glimpse, but he could've sworn one of the women that walked on ahead of him had been wearing a mask. He watched the woman's back, growing steadily smaller in the distance. She wore deep red in the fine fabrics and ruffled skirts of the upper class, and held a black parasol overhead to shield herself from the sun. She walked alone, not glancing back.

Arhyen wanted to race after her, but forced himself to keep an even pace as he strolled away from the entrance to the postmaster's office. He didn't want the woman to realize he was following her until it was too late for her to run, though as he walked, the woman seemed to increase her pace, or was it only his imagination? He hurried along, weaving his way through the crowd. Something white flitted to the ground from the woman's gloved palm. Some sort of note? Did she realize that he followed, or had she lost the paper on accident? Either way, he desperately wanted to see what was on it.

He raced forward to fill the space she'd vacated and crouched quickly to pick it up, then stuffed it into his pocket. He resumed his chase. Moments after he retrieved the paper, the woman glanced back, giving him a clearer look at her mask. It appeared to be the same one the masked man had worn, or else something very similar. It seemed almost lifelike, until closer observation revealed the coloring was a tad too white, and the texture just a bit too smooth to be human skin, not to mention the strange look it gave to the eyes peeking out. She glanced back again and looked directly at Arhyen for a moment, then took off down the sidewalk at a jog. At her quickened pace, the passersby began to take notice.

"Oi!" one man called out as the woman nearly collided with him.

Arhyen began to run, intent on not letting her get away.

She veered right into a nearby shop. Not even taking the time to note what type of shop it was, Arhyen followed in after her, letting the door slam shut behind him with a loud *bang*. The shopkeeper, a middle-aged man with a large belly covered by a white apron, put his hands up in surrender as Arhyen came to a skidding halt in front of his counter. There was a hallway behind the man leading deeper into the building. Arhyen listened as another door opened and slammed shut, somewhere near the end of the hall.

Not bothering to ask for permission, he vaulted over the counter and continued to give chase. He rounded a bend in the hallway, lined with boxes of various goods, then found the door. He flung it open and raced out into the back alleyway, then looked right and left, peering around trash heaps and stacks of wooden crates. The alleyway reeked of garbage, but it barely fazed him. There was no one in sight. The woman had escaped. He listened a moment more, but heard no sound of retreating footfalls.

Heaving a frustrated sigh, he began walking, wanting to put distance between himself and the shop he'd barged through. As he walked, he looked down at the paper in his hand. It read:

LOWFIELD ROAD AND NEWLAND STREET. 10PM. COME alone.

-V

HE PAUSED TO CONSIDER THE WORDS. LOWFIELD ROAD was in the industrial district, if he recalled correctly. Nothing resided there except warehouses and manufacturing plants, mainly for steel. Could *V* stand for Victor? If Victor was associated with the masked man and woman, that would mean *he* had stolen Fairfax's journal. This could all be an elaborate trap to get his hands on Liliana, but if it was, why the extra step? They were already searching for Victor Ashdown. If this was all a ploy to kidnap Liliana, then why did the note say to come alone? If they simply wanted to eliminate the complication he might pose, they could have done it right that moment, while he was standing alone in an alleyway.

That thought got him moving. He would circle back around to the postmaster's office and continue on with his original plan. He needed to find as much information on Victor Ashdown as possible before 10 PM. Once he had that information, he would decide whether or not he would attend the meeting.

He strode forward, thoughts of Victor Ashdown, Fairfax Breckenridge, and the ticking bomb that was Clayton Blackwood on his mind. Underneath it all, were thoughts of Liliana. She didn't deserve to be involved with any of these men. Most of all, she didn't deserve to be involved with *him*.

CHAPTER 8

Liliana bit her lip in concentration as she added the final touches to the freshly written formula. It was the fourth one she had written, and she was quite sure that she had them all correct. Now, if only she knew just what they would create.

Keys turning in the various locks of the door drew her attention. She pushed a lock of red hair behind her ear, glancing at the door apprehensively. Suddenly unsure if she wanted to show Arhyen her work right away, she closed the journal, concealing, but hopefully not smudging, the freshly written page, and placed it in her lap.

The door swung inward to admit Arhyen. He removed his black cap, then looked at her curiously. "Willy is on the lookout," he announced with a smile. At Liliana's questioning gaze, he elaborated, "Willy is a post-man. He's going to attempt to find Victor Ashdown's address for us." He shut and locked the door behind him, then moved to join Liliana on the sofa. As soon as he sat, he glanced down at the journal in her lap. "Any luck?"

Her heart skipped a beat. She felt like she couldn't

breathe. Should she tell him it was done? If he knew she'd the finished journal, things would move forward. She would find out the purpose of the formulae. She took a deep breath. "It's done," she admitted. If she ever wanted to find her purpose, she would first have to learn what she really was.

Arhyen's face lit up with excitement. "Good heavens, you remembered everything?" he asked, sounding somewhat astonished.

She lifted the journal from her lap and handed it to him, then fell silent as he perused the contents. She had only filled the first few pages, but they were the most important. They held the four formulae that Arhyen had originally been seeking.

He frowned as he read what she had written, then looked up at her. "And this is all it takes to create a soul? I don't know much about alchemy, but this all seems so simple."

"I don't know if I really have a soul," she admitted. "That's what my father called it, but in all of my reading I have never been able to figure out what the soul really is. It seems impossible to truly create one." She watched his face carefully, waiting for his reaction. She didn't like admitting that she might not have a soul, but wanted to know what he truly felt about it. If it would dissuade him from working with her, she wanted to know now.

He smiled warmly, surprising her. He closed the journal and placed it on the table, then brushed his dark hair out of his face and shifted his legs toward her on the sofa. "I don't know much about souls, but I can tell you one thing. You are not a normal automaton. You are not a *thing*, or a tool. You are a person. No matter what we find, I will continue to think of you as a person."

She inhaled sharply. How had he known just what she

was thinking? "If I find that I do not have a soul, I fear how *I* will view myself," she explained. "I fear that I will not be deserving of a purpose, at least, not in the way that real people deserve it. I fear that I will have wasted your time, and that I will not be worthy of your training."

Arhyen shook his head. "I'm still not sure you understand what it means to become a thief. I may be one of the best, but it is no grand profession. It is nothing that someone can be worthy or unworthy of."

"I'd like to differ," she argued. "I think it is a fine profession, if it is one chosen by a man like you. I may not have met very many people so far, but you are still the only one that has treated me like my thoughts matter. You are the only one who has offered me food, even though I do not need it, simply because I might enjoy the taste. You are the only one who has offered me a bed, even though I do not require sleep. So, if being a thief means that I will be more like you, then I think it is a fine profession that only the most worthy of people deserve."

Arhyen seemed completely taken aback. He did not speak for a full minute, and instead just shook his head slowly. When he finally spoke, he took her hand. "Here I was trying to cheer you up, but it seems you have cheered me instead. No matter what we find, I will continue to teach you anything you want. If you truly desire to be a thief, I will teach you to be one even greater than I."

Filled with elation, Liliana grinned. She still feared finding out whether or not she had a soul, but if Arhyen could accept her without one, then perhaps she could learn to accept it herself. Perhaps she did not have to live in the darkness, in a place she could simply no longer view as her home.

As soon as he had refilled his satchel with supplies, Arhyen left the apartment with Liliana by his side. The new journal was nestled within his satchel, in an inner pocket that would be difficult to steal from unless someone stole the satchel entirely. No one knew that they had the new journal, but he simply could not risk losing it once again. Besides the journal, he had packed a few other supplies that he only carried in the direst of times.

The first items he'd gathered were small smoke bombs, composed of liquid within tiny glass capsules. Once the glass was broken and the liquid was exposed to the air, they would form clouds of smoke. They were relatively harmless, but could provide cover should he and Liliana need to escape unseen. In addition to the smoke bombs, he had packed little capsules of ink. If they encountered any more of their masked *friends*, he would do his best to stain their masks. This way, he would be able to tell if there was only one mask passed between associates working closely together, or countless masks, worn by a larger network. In addition to the capsules, he had various knives concealed about his person.

They walked down the narrow streets away from his apartment side-by-side. The clouds that had begun to form earlier had multiplied, and the scent of rain was thick in the air, though moisture was yet to fall. He glanced at Liliana as they walked, but she paid little attention to him, likely unaware that he had withheld information from her. Not only would he not tell her about the meeting planned for that night, but he would not tell her what he had learned thus far about Victor Ashdown.

After speaking with Willy, he had visited several apothecaries, hoping to gain further information. Though apothecaries tended to focus on medicine, they were still alchemists of a sort, and alchemists often tended to study each other's materials. Not only had one of the apothecaries known who Victor Ashdown was, she claimed to be his daughter. She had also claimed that her father had been missing for many months, and she had taken over his apothecary in his absence. Still, she had refused to divulge her father's home address, and that was where Willy came in. Even if Victor Ashdown was missing, much could likely be learned from investigating his estate.

Arhyen tensed slightly at the feeling of eyes on his back. He continued walking casually, but glanced over his shoulder just as they took another turn. He could see no one watching them. In fact, he saw no one at all except a vagrant in ratty clothing that appeared to be asleep, his back pressed against the side of a building. On the new street, they passed by a few young street urchins and other vagrants, but none paid them any mind, except to occasionally ask for coin. He was about to pass his original feelings off as paranoia, when someone suddenly appeared at his side.

Liliana let out a little yip of surprise and halted, then seemed to calm herself when she realized it was only Ephraim. Ephraim continued walking, expecting them to fall in stride.

Arhyen took Liliana by the arm, then hurried to catch up to Ephraim's side. Ephraim's short, blond hair blowing back from his face with the ozone scented wind was the only part of his face that moved. His eyes and expression remained impassive, giving nothing away. He stopped briefly to straighten the lapels of his long frock coat, then continued walking.

Arhyen remained silent, waiting for the man to speak. He knew this was no social call. Ephraim only sought him out when he either had information to offer, or was looking for information himself.

"A body was found this morning," Ephraim explained suddenly, his eyes still watching the street ahead of them. "It is believed the man died the night before last. Do you know anything about that?"

Arhyen scoffed as he readjusted his bowler cap on his head. "Why on earth would I know anything about that?"

Ephraim smiled coldly. "Well, upon the dead man's person, we found a note. The note read, *I was killed by Arhyen Croft.*"

Liliana gasped and stopped walking, but Arhyen, his arm still linked with hers, quickly pulled her forward again. "Is this some sort of terrible joke?" he questioned, feigning complete ignorance.

Ephraim smirked. "Not at all. That is truly the note that was found, though I don't quite believe the dead man took the time to write a note to point the Watch in the right direction."

"Well I didn't put it there," Arhyen quipped.

Ephraim glanced at him with a stern expression, then continued walking. "Nor was that my suspicion," he replied. "But you understand why I must discuss it with you."

"Of course," Arhyen replied crankily. "And I imagine the Watch will be wanting to *discuss* it with me as well."

Ephraim was silent as they reached a crossroad, and a gaggle of giggling ladies passed by, leaving a cloud of perfume behind. "You catch on quickly," he stated once the women were out of earshot. "It would not be wise to return to your apartment any time soon."

Arhyen waved him off. "None of them know where I live."

They crossed the wide street and continued down another alley.

"I would not be so sure of that," Ephraim countered. "It

seems some higher members of the Watch have taken an interest in you as of late."

Arhyen's heart sped up. Though he had caught the attention of the Watch on occasion, he had never merited a true investigation. Why would they suddenly be watching him now?

"Someone found and reported Fairfax Breckenridge's body," Ephraim explained. "He was murdered, and there are many interesting theories as to why. Word is, you are somehow involved."

"I didn't kill him, if that's what you're asking," Arhyen sniped.

Ephraim shook his head slightly. "No, but I suspect you know *why* he was killed."

Arhyen was about to say he hadn't a clue, which wasn't *entirely* a lie, when Ephraim stopped walking. Arhyen stopped a heartbeat later. Something was wrong.

"It seems we have company," Ephraim commented calmly.

They had been approaching another cross section in the alleyway. Now that they'd stopped, five men stepped into view, previously hidden by a nearby building.

"Friends of yours?" Ephraim asked.

Arhyen shook his head. He recognized a few of the men. They worked for Clayton Blackwood. Their association was further evidenced by the white strip of fabric tied around their left upper arms, over their various coats. Arm bands were used to distinguish many gangs within the slums, but the wealthy elite were no different. Everyone needed a way to tell thugs apart, else you ended up killing the wrong people.

Keeping his eye on the men, Arhyen pushed Liliana behind him. "If things get ugly," he muttered, "*run.*"

Ephraim bared his teeth into a smile. "Does that go for me as well?"

Arhyen snorted and checked the daggers concealed at each of his wrists. "I didn't think that Ephraim Godwin ran from *anything*."

"He doesn't," Ephraim replied, just as the men charged.

Arhyen drew a dagger from his coat, and Ephraim drew a pistol. Arhyen had seen the weapon before, and knew that it only offered one shot before a tedious reloading session, but one shot was better than none. Ephraim fired into the nearest thug's leg and the man went down, making the fight four to two. Arhyen liked those odds, especially with Ephraim by his side, but it was distracting worrying about Liliana at the same time.

Leaving their wounded comrade behind, the other four men pulled blades and charged. The fact that they had knives and not pistols meant they were just there to rattle Arhyen up, and maybe leave him bruised and bloody in the gutter. Handguns were difficult to obtain if you weren't a member of the Watch, but he knew if anyone could obtain pistols for their men, it was Clayton Blackwood.

Arhyen dodged the first attack as Ephraim sent a man sailing through the air to land in a heap two yards away. Liliana screamed.

He narrowly missed another man's fist as it swung toward his face, turning at the last second to see several more thugs had crept up behind them, all with white strips of fabric around their arms. One man had wrapped his forearm around Liliana's chest from behind, and was attempting to drag her away. She struggled against him, putting up much more of a fight than any would have guessed from such a small woman. Arhyen was unsure how he moved as quickly as he did, but the next thing he knew he was swinging his fist into the jaw of the man who held

Liliana captive. As the man's grip loosened, Arhyen grabbed Liliana by the wrist and tugged her toward him to hold her against his chest.

Ephraim took down another man, knocking him out cold, then rushed to Arhyen's side as the remaining men circled them. "There are too many of them," he commented.

"No need to be negative," Arhyen replied, still holding Liliana close. There *were* too many of them. Normally he would try to go down fighting, but he shuddered to think what would happen to Liliana if Clayton got his hands on her.

Arhyen was about to advise they make a run for it, when a whistle blew from somewhere behind them. He had never been so glad to hear the telltale tone that announced the Watch's approach. Several of the thugs glanced around nervously, then a handful of uniformed officers approached from a side alley near where Arhyen, Ephraim, and Liliana stood.

The man who'd taken hold of Liliana met Arhyen's gaze. "You have until midnight tonight to bring both the formulae and the girl to our boss." With that, the thugs turned and ran.

Ephraim rolled his eyes at Arhyen as the men dispersed. "You could have told me you'd gotten yourself involved with Clayton Blackwood," he whispered. "How am I going to explain *this* to my superiors?"

Arhyen didn't have a chance to answer as the officers who'd saved them approached. Ephraim moved to meet them, speaking to them in hushed tones that effectively left Arhyen and Liliana out of the conversation. Ephraim purposefully guided the men a little farther away. Arhyen's gaze trailed after them, hoping his long-time associate would be able to smooth things over. As an upper level detective, the officers would all defer to Ephraim's judgement . . . hopefully, but he'd still have to explain the situation back at headquarters. People talked, even members of the Watch. Ephraim couldn't let an altercation with a known criminal's men go unreported.

Realizing he still had an arm wrapped around Liliana, he jerked slightly, then released her.

She looked up at him with worried eyes. "Who is Clayton Blackwood? Why does he want *me?*" she whispered.

He frowned. *Why*, indeed. "He's the man who hired me to retrieve your father's journal," he explained, leaning close to her ear to avoid being overheard by the officers still conversing with Ephraim a short distance away. "You were *not* part of that bargain," he continued. "He must have recently been made aware of your existence."

"Is he the man trying to frame you?" she whispered.

He sputtered for a moment. "How do *you* know about framing people?"

She frowned. "I've read numerous mystery novels. A dead man with a note in his pocket pointing to his alleged killer seems like an idea straight from one of those books."

He nodded. "It does indeed, but I do not believe Clayton is the one trying to frame me, if that is really what's going on. He would gain nothing from my arrest, especially when he could easily just have me killed."

"Then who?" she whispered.

Arhyen shook his head. He wished he knew. The first obvious conclusion was the masked man, but why would he lead him on a search for Victor Ashdown if he simply wanted him out of the way? And why would he then invite Arhyen to a meeting that night, if he would be arrested before he could make it? Nothing fit together. Either the masked man was entirely mad, or there were other players in the situation of whom Arhyen was yet to be made aware of.

Ephraim parted ways with the officers, then approached Arhyen and Liliana with a heavy sigh. "I'm going to have to arrest you now," he stated.

Arhyen balked. "I have no time to get arrested. I've too many mysteries to uncover."

Ephraim made a *hmph* sound. "Be that as it may, my colleagues have recognized you." He glanced back at the uniformed men, still waiting where he'd left them. "You'll have to come in for questioning. I cannot risk my reputation by letting you go."

Arhyen clenched his jaw in irritation, but knew he had no choice. If he ran, it would only make him look guilty to the waiting officers. If he cooperated and went in for questioning, Ephraim could likely have him back on the streets within a few hours.

His shoulders slumped. "It's too dangerous to leave Liliana on her own," he muttered in defeat.

Ephraim nodded, then offered Liliana a small smile. It wasn't exactly warm, but from Ephraim, the smile was more than most would ever get. "We'll take her with us. She should be safe enough at the station. Blackwood's men would not dare try to claim her amidst an entourage of officers."

Arhyen sighed in relief. Chances were, he'd end up dead within the next day or so, and Liliana would find herself in the clutches of the masked man, or Clayton Blackwood, but at least neither thing would be happening within the next few hours. Times were exceedingly dire when being questioned by the Watch for murder could be seen as a blessing.

CHAPTER 9

Arhyen leaned his elbows on the rickety table of the interrogation room, supporting his chin with his handcuffed hands as he repeated his story for the millionth time. *He had no idea who the dead man was. He had no idea why there had been a note in the dead man's pocket incriminating him.* They'd even questioned why he had been out of town, which meant they'd done some digging. The only explanation he could think of was that he'd gone to escort his friend, Liliana, back to London. That way, if they tried to question her too, their stories would hopefully match up. He could only keep his mouth shut and hope she wouldn't admit that he was a thief, and she was a thief in training, to any of the officers.

He had no idea if she'd be questioned at all, and in fact, hadn't seen her since they'd arrived at the station, though Ephraim, standing near the closed door, had assured him she would be safe. He also held all of Arhyen's weapons, and his satchel with the new journal and other possessions had been left with Liliana.

The officer questioning him leaned forward across the

table, his paunchy, sweaty face scrunched up in frustration. His tobacco tinged breath assaulted Arhyen's nose as the officer asked once again, "If you have *no* connection to the man we found dead in an alley, not far from where you were spotted at a local cafe, then why was your name in his pocket?"

Arhyen sighed and lowered his cuffed hands to his lap, trying his best to not snap at the infuriating man. "I have no idea who the dead man is," he said honestly. "Nor do I know why my name was in his pocket." Another honest statement, mostly.

Ephraim covered his mouth, silently snickering at Arhyen's frustration, out of view behind the officer's back. Arhyen did his best not to glare at him, then waited for the officer to once again repeat his questions, but they never came. Instead, a sharp knock sounded on the door.

Ephraim moved to open it, and another uniformed officer poked his head in. "A word, please?" the officer asked, gazing at Ephraim.

Ephraim nodded and stepped out of the room with the officer, shutting the door behind him.

Arhyen turned back to meet the glare of the pudgy man across the table.

Several excruciatingly silent minutes later, Ephraim returned to the room. "I'll take care of the prisoner," he stated, his eyes on the pudgy officer. "All men are needed in the Captain's office for briefing."

The officer hopped to his feet, surprisingly agile given his stout stature. Within seconds, Ephraim and Arhyen were alone. Ephraim walked calmly toward the officer's vacated chair and took a seat, then gazed thoughtfully at Arhyen.

"So am I free to go?" he asked hopefully.

"Not quite," Ephraim replied, his emotions impossible

to read. "It seems that several of Clayton Blackwood's men were just found dead. I have not verified that they were the ones who attacked us, but I would somehow not be surprised. Arhyen, what the hell is going on?"

Arhyen blinked at him in shock. "Found dead?" he questioned in disbelief.

"Quite dead," Ephraim assured him. "Butchered, really. Some were only identifiable by the white bands tied around their arms. What's more, is they were found piled near Blackwood's front gate, which as I'm sure you know, is in the well kept, wealthy district of town, so lovingly referred to as White Heights. Most of the residents have security personnel coming out of their ears. Yet, no one saw the killers. The bodies were just suddenly *there*."

Arhyen shook his head, still not entirely able to comprehend what he was hearing. If there was a time to be honest with Ephraim, the time was now. He took a deep breath. "I was hired by Blackwood to retrieve a journal from Fairfax Breckenridge's hidden estate. I had returned from doing just that when we met you at the train station. Not long after entering London, the journal I'd retrieved was stolen from me by the masked man. I've been trying to discern his identity ever since. That same masked man led Liliana and I to a note, allegedly from her father, stating that she should seek out Victor Ashdown. This morning, as I searched for Victor, a masked *woman* dropped a note in front of me, inviting me to a meeting at 10 PM, *tonight*. Honestly, I have no idea who killed Blackwood's men, or why."

Ephraim took a sharp breath, his expression a rare show of surprise. "You *could* have told me all of this sooner," he breathed.

Arhyen shrugged and leaned back against his chair. "You didn't ask."

Ephraim shook his head in reply, but seemed to be deep in thought as he stroked his fingers across his lightly stubbled chin. "Victor Ashdown, you say?"

Heaving a sigh of relief that Ephraim seemed to believe him, he nodded.

Ephraim pursed his lips in thought. "Victor Ashdown was reported missing several months ago by his daughter. We found no leads whatsoever. As far as the Watch is concerned, Victor Ashdown vanished into thin air."

Arhyen nodded. "I spoke to his daughter as well. She refused to give me his home address so I could investigate."

Ephraim raised a pale eyebrow at him. "And you think you'd actually find something the Watch has missed?"

He shrugged, shifting his wrists uncomfortably in the handcuffs. "Perhaps. The Watch likely just looked for signs of *who* had taken him and where he'd been taken to. I'd be looking for signs of *why* he was taken in the first place, if that is indeed what happened."

Ephraim smirked. "Well then let's go." He stood, then moved to unlock Arhyen's cuffs.

His hands freed, Arhyen rose from his chair. "Aren't you needed to investigate a mass murder right about now?"

Ephraim chuckled. "No, I'm beginning to find this case *much* more interesting." He retrieved Arhyen's daggers from the large pocket of his tan overcoat and placed them on the table.

Arhyen shook his head as he retrieved his weapons, wondering if Ephraim was entirely sane. Still, he wasn't about to argue. Officially recruiting a detective of the Watch might well be the biggest break he'd had yet.

LILIANA FIDDLED WITH HER FINGERS NERVOUSLY,

leaning her back against the hard chair. Arhyen had been gone for several hours, leaving her with his satchel and no information on what might happen. The satchel rested heavily in her lap.

The officers milling about the small room had mostly ignored her while she sat there quietly, then a few minutes ago, all but one had rushed out of the room. No one had bothered to tell her what was going on, and now she sat in the empty room with the one remaining officer, who never looked up at her as he furiously scribbled something on a piece of paper.

She had almost convinced herself to get up and search for Arhyen, when a nearby door swung open, admitting both he and Ephraim. Arhyen rushed toward her and took her hand, helping her to stand.

"Let's get out of here," he whispered.

He led her toward the entrance of the building while Ephraim chatted with the last remaining officer. She willingly went with him, her legs feeling stiff from so much time spent in the hard chair. As soon as they reached the busy street, Ephraim caught up to their sides. The clouds had continued to accumulate, and now the air was rich with the scent of ozone. Liliana almost hoped it would rain so they could take a break in a nice cafe somewhere, but it was apparently not to be.

Ignoring Ephraim's appearance, Arhyen looked down at her, practically bouncing with excitement. "We may have a lead on Victor Ashdown. Or at the very least, we now have a way to look inside his home," he whispered, leaning close to her shoulder.

She didn't have time to reply as he placed a hand at the small of her back and hurried her away from the police station. They'd lost the entire afternoon, and now the sun was beginning to sink, not to mention the clouds. People milled about the street, many with shopping sacks in their hands. They entered cafes, laughing and chatting, completely oblivious to the sense of foreboding now plaguing Liliana.

Arhyen placed a hand gently on her arm. She gazed up at him, realizing she had stopped walking. She'd been sitting alone for so many hours, and now things were happening so quickly. She started walking again, forcing herself to focus on the task at hand. It was all she could do to trot alongside her companions, trusting that they at least knew what they were doing.

They hurried away from the chaos of the main street toward what appeared to be a residential district. Most of the homes bordering the street were apartments all stacked on top of each other, though some of the tall buildings seemed to be single homes. They paused in front of one such home, and Ephraim produced a key from his coat pocket.

Liliana glanced at the key, then stared up at gray brick building, wondering if anyone would be inside.

Seeming to have a similar thought, Arhyen asked, "Should we knock?"

Liliana fidgeted on the stoop behind the two men. Was this truly Victor Ashdown's home? If so, why did Ephraim have a key?

"His daughter won't be here," Ephraim explained. "She's taken up residence in the small apartment above her father's shop."

Ephraim inserted the key into the lock and opened the door, then strode inside confidently. Arhyen waited for Liliana to go in ahead of him, then followed, shutting the door gently behind him. The home's interior seemed ordinary with wood floors and pristine, white walls. Liliana was unsure of what she had expected. Victor Ashdown had built himself a mysterious persona within her mind. She had envisioned that anyone involved with her father would live in a secret compound with old books and laboratory equipment strewn about. This home, however, boasted only ordinary looking furniture, a few bookcases, a small kitchen, and a staircase, presumably leading to the bedroom. Remembering that Victor Ashdown had a daughter, Liliana changed her mind to envision two bedrooms upstairs, rather than one.

Leaving her standing near the door, the two men began to investigate. Feeling useless, she approached one of the bookcases and began perusing the labels on the books' spines. Most of the books appeared to be works of fiction, though she saw a few alchemical tomes scattered about. She plucked a familiar one from the shelf and flipped through its contents. It was the twin of one of the more advanced books Arhyen had purchased for her. She replaced the book and grabbed another. This one also seemed ordinary. Feeling silly for thinking she might find something of import on the bookcase, she stepped away with a sigh. Ephraim had ventured upstairs, leaving Arhyen to shuffle through stacks of paper on nearby desk.

Deciding she would be more useful at his side, she began to turn away, then something caught her eye. It was a book titled, *Notes from Above*. It was a work of fiction, one she had read many times before, as the same title resided on her father's shelves.

As she knelt to retrieve the book from one of the lower shelves, Arhyen came to stand at her side. "I don't know what I'd hoped to find . . . " he trailed off, sounding tired.

Liliana was too distracted to reply. She wrapped her fingers around the book's familiar green spine, then lifted it from the shelf.

"What do you have there?" Arhyen inquired, kneeling beside her to get a better look.

She stroked her fingers across the book's cover and its ornate gold lettering, repeating the same title on the spine. "My father had this book," she explained distantly. She opened it to the first page, and a small slip of folded paper fell to the floor.

Arhyen retrieved the paper near his foot, then unfolded it. "The *LN* has discovered everything," he read out loud. "Fairfax, they'll be after you next. I hope this letter finds you in time. Take everything and run. The world is not ready for what we have to offer."

He stared down at the paper, a look of astonishment on his face.

There was the sound of a door shutting somewhere on the second story, then Ephraim descended the stairs. "Nothing out of place," he said. He reached the bottom of the stairs and eyed them curiously, then approached. "Not that I expected any different," he finished dryly.

Arhyen stood and handed the note to Ephraim.

He read it quickly, then looked to Liliana, who still crouched on the floor, book in hand. "Do you have any idea what this means?" he asked, gesturing to the note.

Liliana shook her head and stood. She *wished* she knew what it meant. The note had warned her father that someone was coming for him. Could it be the someone who'd stabbed him? If so, did that someone know of *her* existence?

"The *LN* . . . " Ephraim muttered, drawing her out of her thoughts. "What could it stand for?"

"I'm more interested in what he meant about the world not being ready for what they have to offer," Arhyen stated.

Glancing at the book in Liliana's hands and seeming to patch things together, Ephraim moved his gaze to the bookcase. "How did you know to choose that particular novel?"

Liliana's hands convulsed reflexively around the book. "My father had the same one. I've read it many times."

Ephraim stroked his chin in thought. "So Victor hid a note, hoping that Fairfax would know to look there." He stared at the bookcase for a moment longer. "Search them all," he demanded. "We don't want to miss anything else."

The three of them began pulling the books from the shelf, searching each before replacing them, yet Liliana had a feeling they would find nothing more. She kept her thoughts to herself as she checked book after book. Was Victor referring to the formulae that she had produced in the journal that morning? Was that what the world wasn't ready for? She felt a sinking feeling in the pit of her stomach and couldn't help glancing at the satchel Arhyen carried. If the formulae within the journal had made the mysterious *LN* go after Victor Ashdown and her father, would they come for Arhyen next? If they already knew who Liliana was . . . *what* she was, then it wasn't safe for her to be around him. She should take the journal and leave. If she was then captured, at least whoever wanted her would have no further need to pursue Arhyen. Her thoughts nagging her, she replaced another book onto the shelf. The first opportunity she had, she should take the journal and run. Any other course of action would be selfish. Where she would go, she did not know, but if she left, at least Arhyen and Ephraim would be safe.

THE TRIO LEFT VICTOR ASHDOWN'S HOME JUST AS NIGHT fell. Arhyen felt nervous to be out in the dark streets with such a small group. He had a sneaking suspicion that the

LN had something to do with the masked man, and that the masked man had something to do with Clayton's murdered thugs. Whatever the *LN* was, it was interested in the work of Fairfax Breckenridge. They were likely behind Victor's disappearance, and may have been behind Fairfax's murder. Liliana had claimed that she hadn't seen nor heard anything when her father was killed. She'd simply happened upon him in the hallway, after he'd already gotten a dagger stuck in his back. If the journal was *that* important, and Clayton was after it, it made sense to take out his men. Clayton himself would be difficult to reach, but killing his men sent a very clear message. *End your machinations, or else.*

There was a fresh coating of moisture on the street. Apparently the clouds had expended a bit of their moisture while they'd been snooping around Ashdown's home. He shook his head as they walked down the quiet street, his mind hung up on Clayton Blackwood. He would not give up so easily. He was a man used to getting what he wanted, just as he was used to having little to fear. While most men would heed the warning of several mutilated corpses being left at their gate, Clayton Blackwood would see it as a challenge. He'd be after the journal now more than ever, and by effect, would be after Arhyen.

"I'll look into finding information on the *LN*," Ephraim stated, his eyes scanning the damp empty street ahead of them. "Do you have somewhere to lie low until then?"

Arhyen nodded. "I can think of a few places." He glanced at Liliana. "Though I'm not sure where I'll want to be around 10 PM," he added cryptically, hoping Ephraim would catch on that he had *not* told Liliana about the possible meeting.

"10 PM is a dangerous hour," Ephraim replied cryptically. "I'd not be out at that time without adequate information."

Arhyen glanced at Liliana to make sure she wasn't catching on. If he did decide to go to the meeting, there was no way he was taking her into that sort of danger, especially now. Fortunately, she gazed off distantly, obviously immersed in her own thoughts.

"Yet much could be gained," Arhyen countered.

Ephraim nodded. "In that case, I will go with you."

Arhyen shook his head, then glanced again at Liliana, still deep in her own thoughts. "There are other things that *LN* might want," he explained ambiguously.

"Then I will watch over them," Ephraim assured.

Arhyen nodded in acceptance, relieved that he wouldn't have to leave Liliana alone while he went to the *meeting*. If anything happened to him, Ephraim would keep Liliana safe. He wasn't sure at what point Ephraim had been upgraded from an acquaintance of occasional favors to full-time partner, but he wasn't about to turn down the help of one of London's finest, especially when it felt like the entire city had somehow turned against him.

CHAPTER 10

L iliana glanced at the satchel, then toward the door as she nervously clutched the sides of her hard, metal chair. Ephraim stood with his back to her, searching through a nearby file cabinet. His blond hair reflected the light of the single, dim bulb hanging from the ceiling. They were back at the mostly empty police station. At the late hour, the majority of the other officers were either patrolling the streets, or they'd gone home . . . or so Ephraim had explained to her before turning to ignore her completely. She glanced at the satchel again, lying forlornly at the foot of Ephraim's desk, in his small, dingy office. Any moment now, she would make her escape.

After retrieving a few items from the satchel, Arhyen had left it, and the recreated journal, with them. He'd claimed he was simply returning to his home for supplies, but Liliana was not quite sure she'd been told the truth. His honey colored eyes had shifted slightly as he ordered her to remain with Ephraim.

She glanced at the back of the man in question as he muttered something to himself. Ephraim was looking for information on the *LN,* and she had a feeling Arhyen was doing the same, wherever he was.

She pursed her lips in thought, trying to remember anything she might know, but she was quite sure her father had never mentioned the *LN*, unless it was an acronym, and she simply wasn't connecting the words with the abbreviation. What could it mean? *London Nation, Lawful News, Little Network* . . . her thoughts trailed off.

"Aha!" Ephraim exclaimed, though she was sure he was speaking to himself since his back remained turned. "*London Network*," he muttered.

"*London Network?*" she questioned.

Ephraim startled as if he'd forgotten she was there. He turned to look at her with a stack of papers clutched in his hands. "Yes," he explained, the light of the single bulb illuminating his face eerily. "I knew I had heard the acronym *LN* before." He approached his desk and spread out the papers he'd removed from the filing cabinet. Hovering over them, he continued, once again sounding almost as if he were just muttering things to himself, "We've had several reports over the years of an organization referred to as the *London Network*. A few have claimed that this organization was out for their lives, but they were mainly criminals, so the information was taken down, and not much was done. Over time, we gathered enough reports for the *London Network* to merit its own file, and at that time the Watch looked into the previous cases, but nothing was ever found. As far as anyone can tell, the *London Network* is a myth."

Liliana furrowed her brows, ruminating. "But if they're a myth, what happened to my father, and where is Victor Ashdown?"

Not answering her, Ephraim returned to the file cabinet and opened a new drawer. After flicking through its upright contents, he withdrew a thick stack of papers, clipped together with a photograph on top. He returned and handed the papers to her. "Have a read over those, would you? See if anything jumps out at you."

She looked down at the papers, topped with the photograph, then gasped.

Ephraim turned back toward her, finally giving her his full attention. "Find something already?"

She nodded, then looked back down at the photograph. "I know this man. He visited our home on several occasions." She'd recognize those clever blue eyes and thick moustache anywhere. "His name is Remington Hobbes."

Ephraim moved to kneel in front of her, then flicked the photograph in her lap. "That man is Victor Ashdown," he explained. "This is his missing person's file."

Liliana shook her head. "No, I remember quite clearly. His name is Remington Hobbes."

Ephraim sighed. "He might have told you that was his name, but I assure you, this is Victor Ashdown. This photo was provided by his daughter."

It didn't make sense. Why would Victor Ashdown go by a fake name when only she and her father had been present? There had to be some sort of mistake.

"Look through the rest of the papers," Ephraim suggested. "See if anything else jumps out at you."

She nodded and did as he said, pushing off her plans of escape. She knew she needed to get away from Arhyen and Ephraim to ensure their safety, especially if this *London Network* was after her, but she couldn't resist delving into the mystery that was unfolding before her.

She scooted her chair toward the desk, opposite where Ephraim stood, to hold the papers nearer the office's lone lightbulb. The first sheet was filled with simple descriptors. *Height, weight, address* . . . then she reached a scribbled note at the bottom of the page. *Alchemist credited with the formulation of the Advector Serum.*

Something tickled at the edges of her memory. She pushed the paper toward Ephraim to regain his attention. "What is this?" she questioned, pointing to the scribbled note.

"Ah, yes," he mumbled, reading over the note. Finished, his eyes turned up to her. "Victor Ashdown was mildly famous for this discovery. The *Advector Serum* is a substance created to be mixed with medicines that need to be inhaled. It binds to other serums, turning them into vapor particles small enough to be absorbed through the lining of the lungs. Do you know something about it?"

Her memories came crashing back to her. It was a time before she'd really became *herself.* Her father had been working to create her *soul.* He'd been muttering about it for weeks as she blindly assisted him. The memory was foggy, just like any other memories of that time, but she was quite sure he'd mentioned the *Advector Serum* on numerous occasions.

"I think," she began shakily, then took a deep breath. "I think this is part of what my father . . . " she trailed off, realizing that Ephraim still thought she was Fairfax Breckenridge's *real* daughter, and not an artificial construct. "It was part of a medicine he gave me," she corrected quickly.

Ephraim frowned at her. "Well that's not uncommon. That's what the *Advector Serum* is for, after all. What type of illness did you have?"

The question almost made her laugh bitterly. Her only illness was to be created as a *thing.*

He shook his head. "What am I saying? Automatons can't catch illnesses."

Liliana jumped to her feet in surprise, knocking Victor

Ashdown's file from the desk to land with a *thwap* at her feet.

Ephraim raised an eyebrow at her. "I've known since the beginning," he explained. "I could tell the first night we met that it was your first time coming to London. Then you had dust stains on your shoulders and your lap, like you'd been sitting in place for months. Finally, when I came to see you the next day, after both you and Arhyen had a very late night, you appeared energetic, your face flawless, while Arhyen looked like he'd been dragged through the gutter."

Liliana felt like she might cry. Was she that transparent?

Ephraim didn't seem to know what to do with her change in demeanor. "Most would not notice," he added quickly. "It's simply my job to note the small things, and don't worry, I can tell you're not a *normal* automaton."

She took a deep, shaky breath, resigning herself to what she needed to say next. "My father used the *Advector Serum* to administer a very special type of medicine to me," she explained. "The added substance, he referred to as my *soul*."

Ephraim blinked down at her in surprise, then gazed off distantly with a wry smile. "Oh Arhyen," he muttered, "what *have* you gotten me into this time?"

Liliana wasn't sure what he was talking about. She retrieved Victor Ashdown's file and sat back down with it, not wanting to leave Ephraim with an opening for questions once he'd recovered from the shock of the news. She gazed down at the photograph on top of the papers. *Who are you, Victor Ashdown?* she thought. *And what exactly did you help my father create?*

⚜

ARHYEN HURRIED TOWARD THE MEETING PLACE. HIS

smoke bombs were in his pocket, and he'd equipped himself with several extra blades, a few of which, he'd had to borrow from Ephraim. Also from Ephraim, was the pistol hidden in his long overcoat, just in case. He pulled his bowler cap down to shadow his eyes, and hitched up the collar of his charcoal coat, also borrowed from Ephraim, to obscure a bit of his lower face, preferring to remain unrecognizable to any passersby.

His thoughts remained on Liliana and Ephraim. Hopefully they'd find something useful about the *LN* and Victor Ashdown at Watch headquarters. Arhyen would just need to live long enough to hear about whatever they found. There was a great possibility that the meeting was a trap to simply get him out of the way, but he could not risk missing out if it was not. Despite the casualties, Clayton would surely send more men after him soon. Now that the tycoon wanted Liliana added to the bargain, Arhyen wouldn't be coming through on either end. The new journal, which had remained with Liliana, would never be delivered, and Arhyen would never receive the largest payday of his life. He shook his head as he walked along. It didn't matter. He had a feeling he'd stumbled onto something *much* larger than him, and his main concern now was to get himself and Liliana out alive.

As soon as he was out of the night time crowds, he picked up speed, keeping to the shadows. His feet fell near-soundlessly on the pavement. The meeting would take place in the industrial district. If he recalled correctly, the corner of Lowfield Road and Newland Street played host to a massive steel smelter, surrounded by warehouses for storing the manufactured beams. The area boasted numerous dark alleyways and ominous buildings, most of which had been long since abandoned. It was the perfect place for a clandestine meeting . . . or an ambush.

Nearing the location, he crept to halt and pressed his back against the side of a nearby building, concealing himself in the darkness of an alley. He peeked out at the street corner where he was to meet the mysterious *V*. There was no one there. Perhaps they were waiting in hiding for him to show up, or perhaps they hid inside the manufacturing plant. He could either wait beneath the lone street lamp that illuminated the corner, or investigate the looming building some distance behind, bordered by tall fences topped with spiky wires.

His mind made up, he crept around the corner to approach the smelting plant in a roundabout manner, hoping to see whoever might wait there before they saw *him*. Just as he approached a cross section in the street, he heard voices.

"It's after ten, perhaps he isn't coming," a man's voice whispered.

"He'll come," a female voice assured. For some reason, the voice sounded familiar to him, though he couldn't quite place it.

He waited in the shadows for them to speak again, but the pair remained quiet. Cursing to himself, he silently backed away, then hurried back down the previous alley to loop around to the one where the mysterious people hid. Panting slightly with exertion, he peeked into the new alley. He could barely make out two forms silhouetted by the moonlight, standing amongst the rubble of the alley. They waited near the main road, just far enough back to be concealed by the surrounding buildings, watching the street corner for his appearance. His forehead damp with nervous sweat, he crept forward, taking cover behind various trash pails and other debris, until he was within a few yards of them.

He was about to make a move, when a light caught his eye, flickering near the fence that surrounded the smelter.

"There's no sign of him inside the plant," the woman whispered.

Arhyen froze. They must have had other accomplices watching over the warehouse, and perhaps observing the street corner from other angles. He was lucky he hadn't been spotted. Quickly changing his tactics, he withdrew a dagger from the sheath at his wrist and considered his options. He would have preferred to attack the man, disabling the larger opponent, but the woman was closer. She would have to do.

He crept closer, then rushed forward. He grabbed the woman from behind, pulling her against his chest and placing the dagger against her throat. She was tall for a woman, but Arhyen could still clearly see her male companion over her shoulder.

"Not a word," Arhyen cautioned as the man blinked at him in surprise. The woman wore a cloying perfume that scratched at his memories, but he still couldn't quite place her, and now with their positioning, he had no chance of seeing her face.

"Why Arhyen," she whispered softly, "I knew you were clever, but I honestly didn't expect to find a dagger at my throat."

His eyes widened as realization dawned on him. He *did* know that voice. Rouged lips came to mind, obscured by a haze of tobacco smoke. He'd played poker with her a handful of times, and she'd been present at the game he'd attended with Liliana. What was her name again? He wracked his brain.

"Viola," he whispered, the name finally coming to mind. "I must admit, you are the last person I expected to find waiting in ambush for me."

"Not in ambush," she stated calmly. "We only wanted to ensure that you truly came alone."

"Well I'm here," he replied simply.

The man stood by with a blank expression. Arhyen suddenly realized that he recognized his facial scars and thick neck, atop a massive body. He had manned the door at the same establishment. Arhyen had seen him many times before, though he looked far different in his current black clothing and matching fedora, partially obscuring his bald head.

"We want the journal," Viola said simply, "and we're willing to pay for it."

"Why?" Arhyen asked instantly.

Viola tsked at him, not seeming at all frightened to have a blade pushed against her throat. Perhaps she knew he had no intention of using it. "Does it matter?" she questioned.

"Quite," he replied simply.

She chuckled. "Because of the girl? You know she's not *real.*"

Arhyen had to stifle his surprised grunt. Liliana did a splendid job at passing as *real,* so he found it unlikely that Viola had deduced her true nature during the course of a single poker game. Whoever had informed her about the journal knew just what Fairfax Breckenridge had created.

"Hardly," he lied. "My interests lie with the *LN.*"

He waited for her to stiffen in reaction, but she remained relaxed. If the acronym caught her off guard, he didn't sense it. The lights flickered again from the fence near the smelter. He was probably running out of time before someone came to check on Viola and her companion.

Viola's head turned slightly to glance in the direction of the lights. "And the *LN*'s interests have recently come to lie with you, Arhyen," she explained, laughter in her quiet voice. "If you give us the journal and the girl, you might be allowed to go about your life as before. If not, well, you might just end up like Victor Ashdown. Or even worse, like Clayton Blackwood's men."

Arhyen did his best to keep his breathing steady. She was claiming to be with the *LN*, which he'd assumed was associated with the masked man . . . yet *he* had stolen the original journal, and Viola didn't seem to know that.

Footsteps began to echo toward them down the main street, coming from the direction of the smelter.

"Time's up," Viola taunted.

Arhyen stepped back and withdrew the dagger, just as he reached his free hand into his pocket. He withdrew a glass vial and threw it at his feet. Within seconds, the alley was filled with smoke. He darted back in the direction he'd come, stepping lightly to avoid making sound in case one of them had a pistol. Viola and her companion coughed and sputtered in the polluted confines of the alley, likely thinking of nothing more than the need for oxygen.

Two figures stood at the end of the narrow street to intercept him. Not slowing his pace, he hit them with another smoke bomb. In their surprise, he managed to slip past, and continued running as if his life depended on it, which it probably did. He made several turns down the various alleys he'd scouted out on his way there, being sure not to hit any dead ends. For a while, the sound of numerous footsteps followed him, but eventually he was able to slip away into the night.

It was only when he was almost back to Watch headquarters that he paused to catch his breath. The *LN* had kidnapped, and possibly killed Victor Ashdown. Viola seemed to be taking credit for that, as well as the mass murder of Blackwood's men. It could all be a lie though, especially since she was still looking for the journal.

Perhaps Viola had only been observing what was going on, and was using the acts of others to threaten him. Perhaps she'd encountered the masked man, and had emulated him to pique Arhyen's curiosity. There were too many *perhaps*.

At that moment, the only thing Arhyen Croft was sure of, was that he wouldn't be giving the replicated journal, nor Liliana, to *anyone*.

CHAPTER 11

Liliana jumped as a knock sounded on the outer door of the station. Ephraim left the office to investigate, cautioning her to remain where she was. She looked down at the paper still in her lap, realizing she'd missed her window for escape. She'd become so entranced as she read over Victor Ashdown's file, that hours had gone by without her noticing.

Moments later, Ephraim reappeared with Arhyen at his side. "It seems our young lady knows Victor Ashdown personally," he explained as both men entered the room.

Arhyen gazed down at Liliana in surprise. He seemed tired and slightly shaken. "Why did you say nothing earlier?"

"I knew him by a different name. He visited my father on several occasions," she explained.

"Tell him the rest," Ephraim softly urged.

Liliana gazed down at her hands in her lap, then looked up to meet Arhyen's eyes. "Mr. Ashdown created the serum my father used to give me a . . . soul," she finished hesitantly.

Arhyen stepped forward, then pulled out the desk chair to slump down into it, obviously taken aback. He glanced up at Ephraim. "I'm assuming the two of you had some interesting conversations while I was away?"

Ephraim eyed him blankly. "I was already aware of Liliana's nature, if that's what you're asking."

Arhyen shook his head, an amused expression on his face. "You're a much better detective than I give you credit for."

Ephraim smirked. "So glad you've finally admitted it."

Arhyen shook his head again, then turned his attention back to Liliana. "So you're saying that your father used this serum, along with the formulae in the journal, to give you your . . . " he trailed off, turning his hand in the air as if trying to think of the best word to use.

She nodded somberly, once again recalling the fuzzy memory. "When Ephraim explained to me what the serum was for, I managed to remember something from an earlier time in my life. When my father made me what I am, it was through the inhalation of certain compounds. He told me he was giving me a soul, but I'm no longer sure if that's what he really meant."

Arhyen scooted his chair closer to hers, though he didn't quite meet her eyes. "Are you sure you want to keep looking for answers?" he asked hesitantly. Finally, he turned his gaze up to her.

The look in his eyes was so earnest that she almost ran away on the spot. She thought perhaps she could face the answers she sought, if Arhyen was willing to face them with her, but she knew she could not ask him to do so. She had missed her opportunity for a clean escape, but perhaps it was not too late to save her friend any further trouble.

"I think I would like to take the new journal and go back home," she stated.

Arhyen's eyes widened in surprise. He leaned back in his chair and let out a long breath. Liliana couldn't help but feel like he was leaning away from *her*.

"Where on earth is this coming from?" he questioned, disbelief clear in his tone.

She searched her mind for an excuse. "I can ignore my father's message no longer," she lied. In reality, she would gladly ignore it for the rest of her life, but she could not tell him that. "I am not human, and I cannot live a normal life. I should never have left my home in the first place."

Ephraim watched the exchange silently, his face void of emotion.

Arhyen, on the other hand, seemed to be suddenly filled with rage. He stood abruptly, knocking his chair aside. "Fairfax Breckenridge does not get to decide what you are, or *who* you are. As far as I'm concerned, you're human. You're more human than half the people I've met in this sorry city. If anyone deserves a normal life, it's *you*. What happened to wanting to find your purpose? Was that all just a passing fancy?"

Liliana felt tears dripping down her face. He was so angry, and she couldn't bring herself to meet his eyes. She tried to think of more excuses, but was without words.

Arhyen suddenly knelt in front of her, quickly removing his gloves. He lifted a hand and wiped her tears away, then held his moist hand up to the light. "You see? You are far more human than the rest of us."

Liliana laughed, but it came out more like a sob. "I don't want you to get hurt because of me," she finally admitted, unable to force out any more lies.

"Of course, no one cares if *I* get hurt," Ephraim chimed in.

Arhyen took her hand in his, ignoring Ephraim's remark. "I'm not going to get hurt," he assured. "I did not become the finest thief in London without having a few tricks up my sleeves."

Ephraim snorted and muttered something that sounded like, "Finest thief my arse," but Liliana's attention remained on the man before her.

"Plus," Arhyen continued, "If you left now, you would make me break my promise. You upheld your end, so now I must train you in my profession."

"Oh don't tell me you plan on making the poor girl a thief," Ephraim cut in.

Arhyen smiled mischievously, then glanced back at Ephraim. "Better than a detective," he teased.

"Hardly," Ephraim muttered.

Arhyen turned his gaze back to Liliana and offered a warm smile.

She smiled back, suddenly glad that she hadn't managed to escape. She was still nervous to discover more information than she currently had, but suddenly found she had the strength to move forward. If Arhyen had *that* much faith in her, it would be a direct affront to him for her to not have faith in herself. Perhaps she wasn't a real person, but so what? Maybe she was simply something *more*.

෪෨

THOUGH ARHYEN NO LONGER HAD TO FEAR ARREST, AT least for the time being, he couldn't very well take Liliana back to his apartment. Clayton was likely still looking for him, and now Viola might be too. Since they had been spotted with Ephraim, anywhere he might be expected wouldn't work either.

That left them with only one sensible option. Find an abandoned building, get some rest, then move on. Ephraim had not wanted to join them, but Arhyen had convinced him that it was only practical. Not only might he be in danger if he returned to his home, when he met up with Arhyen and Liliana once more, he'd risk being followed, leading their enemies right to them.

And so it was that the trio ended up in an abandoned warehouse, sharing the space with a few other vagrants. Arhyen kept Liliana close to his side, wanting to cut off any trouble before it happened as the warehouse's inhabitants eyed them curiously.

"If you owed me a lifetime of favors before," Ephraim muttered, "now you'll be working for me in the afterlife. I never thought to be sleeping in such filth in my life."

Arhyen snorted. "Just be grateful that you were not born into this filth. Some of us have not always had a choice in where we sleep."

They entered an empty room within the warehouse, save a few piles of debris, that he instantly deemed their best choice. Without a word, the trio formed beds from blankets stolen from the police station. Hopefully any criminals that were taken in would not miss them.

"I'll take first watch," Arhyen offered, though he was utterly exhausted.

Liliana shook her head, still standing beside him. "I don't actually need to sleep," she reminded him. "It's better if the two of you get fully rested."

Ephraim had already laid down in his makeshift bed. "I'm not going to argue," he grumbled. Within seconds, he seemed to be fast asleep.

Liliana stared at Arhyen, obviously expecting him to follow Ephraim's example.

"I'll stay up with you for a little while," he whispered. "You can tell me once more all you found on Victor Ashdown." He wasn't particularly interested in hearing more after the initial briefing Liliana and Ephraim had given him, but he felt bad making her stay awake alone. He'd already told her and Ephraim what little he'd learned about Viola, leaving out the part that he had gone to meet her on purpose. Liliana had already felt guilty enough for involving him, he didn't need to rub it in by admitting he'd gone to the meeting alone to keep her out of danger.

Liliana nodded and took a seat on her makeshift bed, combing her fingers nervously through her long, red hair. "What will we do in the morning?" she whispered.

He smiled and sat beside her, removing his satchel from across his shoulders to place on the floor. Apparently she didn't feel like talking about Victor Ashdown either. "You and I will seek out Viola and follow her, while Ephraim returns to the police station to see what information he can dig up on her businesses," he explained. He also had a feeling that following Clayton Blackwood might be useful, but they would try Viola first. If it was a choice between remaining close to a venomous snake, or a small angry badger, he'd choose the badger.

"Do you think that she wants to make more automatons like me?" she questioned suddenly. Her large blue eyes refused to meet his as they reflected the moonlight streaming in through the long since broken windows.

He shook his head, not because it wasn't a possibility, but because he couldn't see what Viola would have to gain. He knew little about her, except that she was a business-woman. Her stock was mainly in steel, just like Clayton. Of course, he would not be surprised if she had more nefarious involvements.

"I think she's probably more interested in what *else* could be created with the same science," he explained softly.

Her eyes flicked to him, then moved back to the

window. "I think we should destroy the journal I made for you," she muttered, surprising him.

"But don't you want to find out just what the formulae are for?" he asked.

She shook her head. "Sometimes I do. Sometimes I think that in order to really move on with my life, I need to find out just what I am. Yet, at other times I think I'm better off not knowing, and I think the *world* is better off not knowing. Sometimes I think I should not have been created at all, since I only seem to bring trouble for those around me."

"What you would call trouble, many would call adventure," he comforted. Sure, he'd been risking his life on a regular basis since he met her, but at least it hadn't been boring. His entire lifestyle had been based around the need to make things less mundane. He could've worked in a steel mill, or could have put his particular talents to more noble uses, but as far back as he could remember, he'd been set on becoming the greatest thief in London. He'd accepted the risks of his lifestyle from the start.

Liliana stared down at her hands in her lap dejectedly.

He nudged her shoulder with his. "Rule number one of becoming a thief," he stated, "nothing is ever supposed to be boring. You see, with your existence, you make my life just what is supposed to be. If you cannot handle that, then perhaps you are not cut out for my profession."

She turned her gaze toward him, now listening intently. "What else?" she asked.

He furrowed his brow in confusion. "What else?"

"The rules of becoming a thief," she clarified.

Arhyen paused in thought. He lifted a finger into the air. "So, we already know rule number one," he began, "and now we must move on to rule number two, which is to never steal from someone who cannot afford the loss."

Liliana narrowed her gaze in thought. "I'm not quite sure I understand."

He gestured to the room around them. "Well, we wouldn't steal from anyone who lived here, would we?"

She shook her head, seeming to catch on.

"But someone like Viola," he continued, "well, she could afford to be taken down a few pegs."

"Rob from the rich and give to the poor," she quoted. "I believe I've read about that in a book."

He had the grace to look abashed. "Well more like rob the rich and give to . . . *us*."

Liliana's mouth formed an *oh* of understanding. "And what's rule number three?" she pressed.

He smiled at her as the final rule came to mind. "Rule number three is to find a partner you can trust. Someone you can rely on to watch your back. Honestly, I only just recently accomplished number three."

She cocked her head, tossing her long, red hair over her shoulder. "Ephraim?"

His laugh hit him so suddenly that he started to cough.

She stared at him like he'd suddenly sprouted an extra head. Did she truly believe he'd trust a man like Ephraim with his life?

Once he recovered, he patted her shoulder and explained, "No, not Ephraim. He'll probably arrest me tomorrow. I was referring to *you*."

Her eyes widened. "You trust *me*? Isn't that supposed to take many years?"

He shook his head. "I'm an excellent judge of character, so I get to skip forward a bit."

She looked down at her lap, seeming to think long and hard on what he'd said. Finally, she turned toward him once more. "I trust you too."

He was pretty sure it was the first time those words had

ever been directed at him. "Don't say that just yet," he advised with a wink. "Wait until I've earned it."

"And how will I know when you've earned it?"

He thought about it. "I'm pretty sure you'll just *know*."

She nodded curtly. "Alright. I'll let you know when it happens."

He laughed. He felt half asleep as they continued to converse, but found himself simply not ready to go to bed until much later that night. Eventually Ephraim awoke, and Liliana was able to sleep too. It didn't matter if she needed it. She deserved as much consideration as anyone else.

CHAPTER 12

The next morning, after waiting at a small cafe for Ephraim to return from the police station, Arhyen had a freshly written list in his hand. Ephraim had obtained information on all of Viola's businesses, as well as her home address. Her file was near bursting with information, not the file of an average citizen. Apparently, she was under suspicion of running illegal gambling rings, and many of her businesses were likely a front to hide her smuggling activities. Under the Queen's rule, taxes on intoxicants had grown high, so smuggling was a common occurrence, though it seemed Viola was smuggling more than spirits, judging by the volume of spotted shipments. Arhyen could personally attest to the validity of the gambling claims, since he'd attended one such game . . . although he hadn't realized Viola was the one running it. Her steel mills seemed to be legitimate businesses, but then again, there was enough money in steel with the expansion of the railroads to eliminate the need for an illegal boost.

As Ephraim left them, Arhyen scooted his chair closer to Liliana's so they could peruse the list together. She'd gathered her red hair into a bun at the nape of the neck, fitting neatly under a black fedora, complimented by a black wool coat with a high collar, both courtesy of Ephraim, in an attempt to hide her identity from any who might recognize her. Her green dress peeked out underneath the coat, but she otherwise looked like a standard lady in mourning, though the hat had far fewer frills than what most women preferred. The clothes wouldn't do much if whoever searched for her saw her face, or the red hair beneath her hat, but they were a start.

They sat in the far corner of the establishment, both with their backs to the striped wallpaper so no one could sneak up on them. Arhyen felt that perhaps he was being a bit paranoid, but after all that had happened, he also felt no one could blame him for being cautious. The murders of Clayton's men had him especially on edge. It would take a large force to not only slaughter so many men, but to then covertly move the corpses through heavily populated areas. Never mind that it had all occurred midday.

No, there was no doubting that the murders had something to do with Arhyen and Liliana. It was too large of a coincidence for so many men to be killed shortly after Liliana's attempted kidnapping, but why go to such an extent? Would the newly dead men also have notes in their pockets incriminating him?

Arhyen sighed and attempted to focus on the task at hand. Shoulders pressed together as they sipped their cooling tea, he and Liliana both read down the list of businesses, more interested in locations than Viola's alleged crimes. The list started with her steel manufacturing plants. As suspected, the plant that had been near the street corner where Arhyen was supposed to appear the previous night belonged to V. Walmsley, the name Viola listed for all of her businesses. Underneath the manufacturing plants were listed several shops and a cafe, the name of which Arhyen recognized. He actually liked the particular cafe, and found himself disappointed that it was owned by the woman who was fast becoming his nemesis.

"This cafe is only a short walk from here," he explained softly, pointing to the name on the list. "We can start there, then check her home address. If she's not present at either location, we'll ask around at the shops."

Liliana nodded, her blue eyes still scanning up and down the list as if she'd memorize it. "What if she finds us first?"

Semi-avoiding her question, mostly because he wasn't sure of the answer, Arhyen turned his gaze downward and straightened the cuffs on his dirty pinstriped shirt, attempting to quiet his nerves. His black pants were stained with patches of dirt, though he'd done his best to brush them off. Ephraim hadn't deigned to bring *him* any new clothing. He took an inordinate amount of time fiddling with his clothing, trying to think up something comforting to say. Finally he straightened the black bowler covering his messy hair.

Liliana waited patiently, giving him a blank stare.

He sighed, seeing he was not going to get off the hook. "If she finds us first, we'll deal with it. I won't let her harm you."

She continued to stare at him evenly. "Will you harm *her*?"

He cringed. Would he harm another woman to protect Liliana? The answer was simple, but he feared what Liliana might think of him. "I will do what it takes to keep you safe," he said softly.

Liliana blinked at him for a few seconds, then nodded. "Okay."

Arhyen folded the list and stuffed it in his waistcoat pocket, then downed the remainder of his tea.

Divining it was time to go, Liliana scraped her fork across her empty plate, scooping up the last remnants of crumbs and icing that were left of her piece of chocolate cake.

Arhyen stood and offered her his hand. She took it and rose. They left the cafe wordlessly and emerged out onto the gloomy street. There was a harsh chill in the air that day, accompanied by billowing smoke flowing from the rooftops as everyone tried to stay warm. The smoke melded with fog and growing clouds, making the sky gray and murky.

Wishing he had a coat, Arhyen instinctively patted his satchel. He'd likely never fully get over being robbed by the masked man, when *he* was the one who was supposed to do the robbing. He briefly considered stopping by his apartment for more appropriate clothing and to stash the journal, but didn't dare. Between Clayton and Viola's men, there were simply too many eyes about, and he would not be surprised if someone riffled through his apartment while he was away. Hence, the journal would remain on his person, and Liliana would remain by his side.

Keeping her close, he guided her down the street toward their first destination. Viola's cafe wasn't far off.

He eyed the occasional passersby warily as they walked. He preferred to spot Viola before she spotted them, but either way, finding her was the primary goal. Now that they'd exhausted their efforts on Victor Ashdown, she was one of the last threads of information they had to follow. They rounded a street corner where the cafe loomed over them. It was an odd time of day, too late in the morning for the breakfast crowds, and too early for those out to lunch. The sparsely populated streets made Arhyen and Liliana easily identifiable to any who might be watching. He tugged his hat down to shadow his eyes, then continued onward.

They approached the large glass windows of the cafe, peering inside to see if Viola was present. Arhyen instantly balked. She was sitting at a table right by the window, sipping tea as if she hadn't a care in the world. He had not expected to find her so easily. It looked like most of Ephraim's work would go to waste. Now the real decision was whether they would follow her, or investigate her home address while they knew she was away.

Deciding that someone who had basically built herself a small Empire, and who'd managed to involve herself in the mystery surrounding Fairfax Breckenridge and Victor Ashdown, wouldn't likely leave evidence floating around her house, he decided it best to follow her as soon as she left the cafe. Perhaps she'd lead them to the *LN*'s secret hideout.

He quickly pulled Liliana into a nearby alleyway to wait before Viola could spot them. From there, they would be able to peek out and witness as she departed, and hopefully remain undetected.

"Do you think she saw us?" Liliana whispered, standing a hairs-breadth from him in the alleyway. Her height put her eyes around his collarbone, forcing her to crane her neck upward to look at him.

He glanced around to verify that they were alone. He could hear the scuffling of a few rats, but the alleyway was otherwise quiet. "I doubt it. That woman seems to think she's invincible. She'd never guess that we'd follow *her*."

Remaining eerily still, Liliana turned her gaze out toward the busy street. They were obscured by the cafe's waste bins, though if someone happened to peek their head down the alleyway, they would be easy enough to spot. Yet being spotted was not what consumed Arhyen's mind in that moment. Liliana's closeness made him nervous for several reasons. First, he feared she'd be better off *nowhere* near him. He was inevitably putting her in danger by following Viola. Given both she and Clayton Blackwood wanted to get their hands on her, hiding Liliana would have been wise. Of course, it was a moot point. He'd been unable to bring himself to leave her somewhere, even with Ephraim. The only way he could truly ensure her protection, was to remain by her side. As for the second reason he was nervous, well, he wasn't quite ready to admit it, even to himself.

His thoughts were interrupted as the bell on the door to the cafe jingled. A lone pair of high-heeled boots sounded on the sidewalk a moment later. Viola had been the only single woman within the sparsely populated cafe, so chances were, the boots belonged to her.

"Let's go," he whispered.

Liliana nodded, her expression determined.

He took her hand and peeked around the corner. Viola's crimson jacket-clad back could be seen as she strolled away in the other direction. He waited a few more heartbeats, then stepped out of the alleyway, with Liliana trailing behind him.

They followed her down the street, stopping as she visited several shops, seemingly running errands. None of it seemed nefarious, but he had no doubt she would eventually lead them to *something*.

The adventure continued.

A few times, Viola glanced over her shoulder, but as the hours wore on and the streets became more heavily populated, it was easy to dodge her line of sight. Eventually, she stopped for lunch. They waited, hidden in a nearby alleyway. Arhyen's stomach growled and his mood turned foul, resentful that Viola was eating fine food while he starved in a scummy alley.

When she finally left the restaurant, they continued to tail her. This time, rather than continuing with her mundane tasks, she walked on through the busy streets, heading in the direction of the residences that composed White Heights. As they continued onward, she became more difficult to follow, since the crowds that had hidden them so effectively remained where there was food and shopping.

They were forced to fall back where they could hide from sight around street corners. Fortunately, Viola did not go far before stopping. They watched from behind a large shrub some distance away as she waited outside a pair of grand gates, tapping her foot impatiently on the pavement. Soon enough, the gates opened before her with a hiss of steam. She confidently marched up the long, gravel driveway.

Liliana's hand in his, Arhyen hustled a little further down the street to hide behind another shrub, this one pruned into the shape of a hunting dog, where he'd have a better line of sight. Liliana pressed close to him, a necessity for them both to remain hidden behind the ridiculous vegetative ornament.

From the new vantage point, they were able to watch Viola as she stopped at the front door of the mansion. Though Arhyen could just barely make out the door opening from that distance, he imagined the automaton maid's impassive face as she invited Viola inside. Soon Viola disappeared into the building. Though there was nothing left to see, there was plenty to think about. The mansion belonged to none other than Clayton Blackwood. What the hell was Viola doing walking into Blackwood's estate?

If he'd been alone, he would have been tempted to

investigate further, but it was too risky with Liliana along. He was about to tell her they should find a more secure hiding place to wait, when movement near the mansion caught his eye. Looking to it, he saw a man dressed in black, with a white mask obscuring his face. He was running alongside the house toward the back.

Liliana, who'd also spotted the masked man, turned wide eyes to Arhyen. Then, much to his surprise, she darted from their hiding spot and effortlessly vaulted over the low wall that encircled the rest of Clayton's estate. After recovering from his shock, he quickly crossed the street, then scaled the wall to chase after her. It was complete insanity running across Clayton's front yard after the masked man, but he couldn't very well allow Liliana to go after him alone. His feet slipping on the damp grass, he pushed himself to run faster. His satchel thunked against his side with each step.

Twenty paces ahead of him, Liliana reached the side of the house where the masked man had disappeared, then hurried around the corner without hesitation. Cursing under his breath, Arhyen followed. He rounded the corner where she'd disappeared, reaching the back end of the house. Liliana had paused there. He stopped too quickly in the slick grass and almost slipped, then recovered and moved to stand by her side. Together they watched the masked man vault through an open window into the mansion.

Arhyen shook his head in disbelief. "Well he's obviously not working *with* Viola," he muttered.

Liliana crept forward, as if she might follow the masked man through the window, but Arhyen grabbed her arm. Realization of the danger she'd put them in flashed through her suddenly worried gaze. "I'm sorry!" she whispered, glancing frantically around the yard. "I can't believe I just ran off like that."

Arhyen calmly followed her gaze around the property. The perfectly manicured lawn and ornate shrubbery surrounding them were utterly still. A fountain larger than Arhyen's kitchen burbled happily nearby, but there were no signs of life. Normally there would be *someone* walking around such a large estate, especially in White Heights were everyone hired security, but perhaps Clayton had lost more of his men than Arhyen had realized. He was obviously understaffed. Still, it would not take long for someone to happen by and notice them.

"We should get out of here," he whispered, still holding onto Liliana's arm.

"I can't let you do that," a voice said from behind them.

They both whipped around to face the owner of the voice, beholding a woman in a maid's uniform. Arhyen recognized her as the female automaton who'd answered the door upon his last visit, when he was trying to buy more time with Blackwood. The automaton eyed them blankly from beneath blonde bangs.

"We were just leaving," Arhyen explained to her. When she just continued to stare, he added, "We got lost."

Their conversation was interrupted as the masked man hopped back out of the large, open window, so near them Arhyen could have grabbed him had he not been completely taken aback. The man took off at a run, faster than anyone should be able to travel on foot, toward the back end of the property. He'd held some sort of parcel in his arm, though Arhyen hadn't the chance to make out what it might be.

The automaton maid turned her head, her gaze strong on the masked man, but made no move to follow.

Shouting echoed from within the house, followed by thundering footsteps hurrying down an interior staircase.

"That's our cue to leave," Arhyen announced quickly.

He tugged Liliana's arm and took off in the direction the masked man had gone, betting he had a well planned escape route. The automaton did not follow, but the shouts and footfalls of others did. Liliana pulled out of his grasp and quickly began to outpace him, following the path the masked man had taken.

Another wall came into sight, composed of solid stone and *much* taller than the wall that had lined the front.

"We'll never make it!" he shouted.

"Yes we will!" Liliana shouted in reply.

"There's no way!" he yelled back, huffing with exertion. The wall was twice his height. Perhaps he could boost Liliana on over, but he'd then have to find another way out.

"Trust me!" she called.

Well he *had* told her that he trusted her. He couldn't very well go back on the statement so soon. They closed the final distance to the wall, with Liliana a bit ahead, as their pursuers gained ground behind them. The masked man was nowhere in sight. He must have found some way over the wall, unless he was still hiding somewhere on the property.

Liliana stopped in front of the wall. "Step into my hands," she uninstructed hastily, bending her knees and linking her hands together, providing a foothold to boost him up.

"Absolutely not," he blurted. "I'll boost you over, then I'll find another way out."

Arhyen glanced over his shoulder as Clayton came into sight in his white suit, followed by Viola and several other men.

"*Trust* me," Liliana rasped, panic clear in her voice as her blue eyes bore into him.

Oh hell, he thought. He placed his foot in her waiting hands and before he knew it, he was thrust upward toward the top of the wall. He barely managed to catch hold of it, then pulled himself up to straddle the top. He turned back, prepared to reach down and pull Liliana up, but there was no need. She had moved to get a running start just as Clayton neared, then flung herself upward like a small agile cat. Suddenly she was atop the wall with him, and continued down the other side as he watched in awe.

With Clayton's angry shouts spurring him on, Arhyen lowered himself down on the other side of the wall to join Liliana. They each nodded to each other, then continued to run, leaving behind the sound of Clayton and Viola arguing over who would be boosted over the wall first.

Liliana sprinted beside Arhyen down the narrow, residential street, laughing gleefully.

"Are you actually enjoying this?" he panted in surprise. Perhaps she had lost her mind.

"It's exciting!" she giggled back.

He shook his head and pressed himself to run faster. The first raindrops began to fall, stinging his eyes from his momentum. Liliana was grinning with one hand raised to keep her hat on her head. She didn't seem to mind the rain, nor the near-death experience. Perhaps she'd make a good thief after all.

THEY RAN UNTIL ARHYEN'S LEGS COULD NO LONGER carry him, though Liliana seemed no worse for wear. They'd made it all the way back to the industrial district, near the outskirts of where the busy shops and cafes began. Not wanting to remain out in the open, but also unable to run any further, Arhyen turned into what was once a nice park, but had been long since left to disrepair. The grass was overgrown, and the trees scraggly and half dead, but it was bordered by buildings on two sides, so Arhyen would at least be able to see someone coming with only having to keep his eyes on two streets.

He made his way across the grassy lot, then slumped down onto a rusted iron bench. Liliana watched him curiously, not seeming fatigued in the slightest. Feeling somehow inadequate, he patted the damp bench beside him, inviting her to sit.

She joined him, then turned to look him up and down. "Are you well?" she questioned.

He removed his hat as the rain began to drizzle again. "It seems I can't quite keep up with your physical prowess," he joked wearily.

She gasped. "I hadn't even thought about it, I'm sorry. I don't tend to tire like normal people."

"You can also jump much higher than normal people," he chuckled, thinking back to the image of her leaping to the top of the wall.

She looked down at her lap, seeming embarrassed.

He tilted his head, attempting to put himself in the line of her vision. "It's a *good* thing," he comforted. He leaned back and looked up at the gray sky. "Let's recap what we've learned today."

She glanced over at him curiously. The rain was beginning to soak through her coat and the cap on her head. Arhyen knew they should soon seek shelter, but the rain felt good on his over-exerted body, and Liliana didn't seem to mind.

He cleared his throat. "First, if you would have given me a chance to explain before running off after the masked man, that mansion was the home of Clayton Blackwood. He's the man who hired those thugs to abduct you," he explained. "Viola had claimed that she was the one responsible for the murder of Clayton's men, yet she's obviously working with him. So either she is secretly planning to cross him, or someone else is responsible for the murders."

"But who?" she questioned. The rain had now dampened her face, and glinted on her skin as her cheek caught a small ray of sunlight peeking through the clouds.

Arhyen lost his train of thought for a second. "Um," he began, then lifted a finger into the air, "oh yes. My bet is on the masked man."

She nodded. "What do we do now?"

"We find out what Clayton and Viola are up to," he replied. "The masked man is obviously interested in them, so if we find out *their* plans, perhaps we will find out his. I didn't tell you this before, but I encountered Viola once, wearing the same mask as our mysterious *friend*. She, at the very least, knows about him, and maybe is even involved with him in some way. Perhaps she truly is planning to cross Blackwood, and is working with the masked man to do so. *But-*" he cut himself off as he fully wrapped his thoughts around the situation.

"But?" Liliana questioned.

Arhyen frowned. "That doesn't explain why the masked man wanted to lead us to Victor Ashdown, or why Viola is still after the journal, when the masked man already has it, unless it's a triple cross. Viola is working with Clayton with the intention of crossing him, while the masked man is working with Viola, fully intending to cross *her*. The masked man started us on a search for Victor Ashdown, likely already knowing that he was missing. Viola is claiming credit for Victor Ashdown's disappearance too. We can confidently state what both Viola and Clayton are after, and so, can predict their moves to some extent, but what is the masked man after?"

Seeming to catch on, Liliana pursed her lips in thought. "He already has the journal, and seems to have no desire to capture me."

He nodded. The rain began to collect in his hair to drip down his nose. He wiped at it absentmindedly. "So the most logical step toward finding out just what *he's* after, is to find out just what those formulae will create."

Liliana frowned. "We'll need a skilled alchemist for that. I understand the formulae in theory, as in, I know which compounds are needed, but I don't think I have the skill to actually create each recipe. Even if I could, we'd still just have an unknown compound. We'd have to use it on someone or something to know just what it does."

"But would a skilled alchemist be able to decipher what the formulae will create just by looking at them?" he pressed.

She sighed and tilted her head, dripping water from her cap. "No, probably not. Most of alchemy is comprehended by *doing* it. Once you know what formulae will lead to a certain compound, you can replicate it. But when creating an unknown formula, you simply have to test the results."

Arhyen nodded. "So we test them."

Liliana shook her head. "But these formulae allegedly created my *soul*. It doesn't seem wise to test them without knowing the possible consequences."

He shrugged. "Well the only other possibility is to ask Clayton or Viola, but I don't think we'll gain any answers *that* way. All we'll gain is a short trip to the grave."

Liliana slouched against the bench with a sigh. He really should have gotten her out of the rain much sooner. She was absolutely soaked.

"Come on," he instructed, returning his cap to his head. "Let's find some place to lie low until the rain dies down."

She nodded, and he stood to offer her a hand up. Her gloved hand felt so small and fragile in his, though he was beginning to realize that she was twenty times tougher than he'd ever be, both physically and emotionally. He paused to wipe a damp strand of wet hair off her cheek. She looked up at him, her blue eyes wide. Yes, she was strong, but she was also lost, just like him.

CHAPTER 13

Not long after Liliana and Arhyen began walking away from the park, the sky seemed to open up entirely, and they were caught in a torrential downpour. They ran, hand in hand, as water began to flood through the streets. The streets were void of life, all of London's citizens having retreated from the rain. Liliana couldn't help her grin. Her father had never allowed her to go out in the rain. Now she was running through the streets of London, splashing through the gathering water, hand in hand with someone who treated her not only like a person, but like an equal. It was exhilarating.

Arhyen took a sudden turn, pulling her along, then stopped in front of a familiar building.

Liliana looked up at the tall, gray brick home in surprise, lifting her hand to shield her eyes from moisture. "What are we doing here!" she called over the thunderous sound of the rain. They were standing directly in front Victor Ashdown's home.

With his free hand, Arhyen dug through his satchel and produced a key. "This is probably one of the last places

Viola or Clayton would look for us," he explained loudly. "I swiped the key from Ephraim's office."

Liliana stared at him wide eyed. "Isn't going in there against the law?" she questioned.

Arhyen chuckled. "Says the girl who wants to become a thief."

She bit her lip, supposing he had a point.

They hurried up the steps and unlocked the door, then retreated from the rain.

Liliana breathed a sigh of relief as Arhyen locked the door behind them. The home was just as empty as the first time they'd visited. It appeared that nothing in the space had been moved since then. They should be safe, at least for a time.

Standing in the entryway beside her, Arhyen extended a dripping-wet arm and removed the cap from her head, placing it on a coat rack near the door where he had placed his own. He then helped her out of her coat, hanging it beneath the hats. She plucked out the pins that now barely held her hair into a bun, then pushed the stray damp strands back from her face, glancing around warily.

Arhyen stopped near the door to light the furnace, then moved to sit on the plush green sofa against the far wall, keeping his satchel with him. The man truly never went without the belonging.

"You're getting it all wet," she chided, approaching him to gesture at the sofa.

He smirked. "Well short of taking off my clothes, there's nothing I can do about that."

Liliana found herself suddenly staring down at her feet in embarrassment. Her dress dripped a steady stream of water onto the ornately patterned carpet. She gasped and stepped away onto the bare wood floor.

She caught Arhyen's eye as he smiled and shook his head at her. "It's just water. It will dry."

She frowned, forcing her chin up. Perhaps the water would dry, but she'd feel oddly guilty if anything got ruined. Wanting to draw attention away from the fact that she was still standing, she questioned, "What do we do now?"

He shrugged and slouched down against the couch, making himself comfortable, though his wet shirt likely lessened the efficacy. "We wait out the rain, then we seek Ephraim."

Liliana fiddled with the wet sleeves of her dress, feeling suddenly nervous. She tried to tell herself it was because they were in Victor Ashdown's home, but she felt it probably had more to do with the fact that she was soaking wet and alone with Arhyen, and there was only one sofa to sit on.

He patted the sofa beside him. "It will dry," he assured at her hesitant look.

She really would have liked to shuck the wet clothing. Her dress was thoroughly soaked despite the shelter of her coat, but there was no way she was doing that with Arhyen in the room. She approached the sofa and sat down uncomfortably, spreading her soggy skirts beneath her.

Arhyen visibly relaxed now that she was sitting, though underneath his easy expression he seemed utterly exhausted. Dark purple bags lined the bottom of his honey-colored eyes, and he was a little paler than usual. His hair dripped a slow stream of water down onto his face that he didn't seem to notice.

He pushed his hair back, flinging water aside, startling her with his sudden movement. "We really should find a way to dry off," he commented. "Perhaps Ashdown's daughter left some of her dresses here. You could wear one."

"I can't steal one of her dresses!" she squealed, surprised by the suggestion.

Arhyen's eyes widened, then he laughed. "Really, you must tell me, what is it that you think thieves *do?*"

She shrugged, then nestled a little more comfortably against the sofa. The furnace was beginning to warm the building, and would hopefully help to dry her clothes. "They steal alchemical journals, and ancient artifacts from hidden temples."

He raised an eyebrow at her. "I'm guessing your father had some adventure novels to go along with the mysteries?"

She looked down, embarrassed.

He touched her cheek, bringing her gaze up to meet his. He seemed about to say something, then suddenly averted his gaze. "I'll make us some tea," he said quickly, then withdrew his hand. He stood and strode away from the sofa into the kitchen, leaving Liliana confused and still a bit embarrassed.

Victor Ashdown's kitchen, open to the rest of the room, was a little more replete than Arhyen's, with a full-sized stove, ice box, wide porcelain sink, and thrice the number of storage cabinets. She watched from the couch as he filled a copper kettle with water, then placed it on the stove. Not glancing in her direction, he began searching through the nearby cupboards, presumably for tea.

Feeling anxious, she rose and journeyed into the kitchen area to aid him. She had only opened her first cupboard when Arhyen let out a low whistle. She looked to him curiously.

He glanced at her, then back to the cupboard. "Come here a minute?" he asked.

She joined him and peered into the cupboard to find neatly stacked plates on the lower shelf, and tea cups, turned upside down to keep out the dust, on the upper shelf. Confused, she looked back to him.

She watched as he reached in and lifted one of the cups. Underneath it was a large gemstone, almost too large for the cup to have covered it. Its deep green facets reflected the light as Arhyen set the cup aside and lifted the gem into his hand. He held it up to the light and peered through it.

"Now what do you suppose that was doing in there?" he questioned distantly.

Liliana stared up at the gem in awe. It was lovely to look at, but difficult to identify. Her father had possessed numerous volumes on geology and the study of minerals, since many could be used in alchemy, but she could not recall any gemstones with such an odd and lustrous hue. Deciding to focus on more pertinent questions, she asked, "What should we do with it?"

Arhyen continued to gaze at the gem. "Rule number four of becoming a thief," he muttered. "Never leave behind a giant gemstone, if you can help it."

Liliana cleared her throat and glared at him.

"What?" he asked, as if she were being absurd.

She continued to glare. It wasn't right to steal Victor Ashdown's gemstone, even if the man himself was missing.

Arhyen sighed and lowered the stone. "We at least should figure out what type of stone it is, and why it was hidden in his cupboard. It may help us to piece together the rest of this mystery."

She nodded curtly. "Then we'll hand it over to Ephraim."

"Why do you trust him more than you trust me!" he exclaimed.

Liliana laughed, wondering why she had ever felt

nervous to be alone with him. "He's a detective. He'll do the right thing with it."

Arhyen sighed. "Fi-ine," he agreed, stretching out the word as if it pained him to say it. "We'll still have to take it with us for now."

She nodded in agreement. She had no idea how they were going to find anything out about the stone, but she knew Arhyen would think of a way. He seemed capable of coming up with plans for *everything*.

The water in the kettle began to steam, making her realize she had yet to find the tea. She resumed her search as Arhyen switched off the burner, finding several porcelain canisters of tea in a cabinet near the sink. They prepared their beverages in companionable silence, then moved back to the sofa, tea cups in hand. Liliana's dress had dried to the point where it no longer dripped, though it was still rather uncomfortable. Still unwilling to search through Victor's daughter's wardrobe, she ignored the discomfort and sat.

Arhyen glanced past her toward the curtained window. "It looks like the rain has let up."

She followed his gaze to see the sun barely peeking through the edge of the curtains. Though it would soon be dark, with the rain gone, she assumed they would head out to find Ephraim. Finding herself almost disappointed that the quiet moment might soon come to an end, she sipped her tea to hide her expression.

"We should still probably stay the night here," he announced, prompting her to glance over at him.

She took another sip, suddenly enjoying the aromatic beverage more than she had before. "All right."

He raised an eyebrow at her. "No arguments?"

She shook her head, hiding her smile. "You said it yourself, this is probably the last place anyone will look for us, and you need a place to rest."

He lowered his tea as his shoulders slumped. "You know, it's a bit emasculating to always be around someone who is not only physically stronger than you, but that doesn't need to sleep."

She cocked her head, not fully understanding his sentiment. "I could sleep too, if that would make you feel better."

He laughed ruefully. "I think forcing you to sleep just because I have to sleep probably makes me even less manly, not more." He paused for a moment. "But we could always lie down and chat for a while."

Liliana's eyes widened. Was he suggesting they lie in the same bed?

He held up his free hand in a soothing gesture. "I wasn't suggesting anything inappropriate. I simply enjoyed conversing with you last night, and thought we might do it again."

Liliana managed to calm herself at his explanation, then nodded. "That sounds nice."

He offered her an easy smile, then took a big gulp of his cooling tea. "Let's check the bedrooms upstairs."

With a nervous glance at the front door, she gave an approving nod. She quickly finished her tea, set the cup on the low table in front of the sofa, then followed Arhyen as he made his way toward the stairs. Though she looked forward to another conversation, she really hoped he would actually get some sleep. She suspected that he'd been pushing himself far too hard over the past few days, and felt guilty because it was all her fault.

There was a short hallway at the top of the stairs with three closed doors. Arhyen opened the first, which appeared to be a normal bedroom. He left that room, and went for next door, revealing another bedroom, this one done in softer, more feminine hues than the first. Though they'd already found two suitable bedrooms, he went for the third, explaining, "Just in case."

She nodded, wanting to see what was behind the door as well. If it had only been Victor and his daughter living in the apartment, there would have been no need for a third bedroom. Arhyen opened the door. They peered together into the room's dark interior, and Liliana realized the term *room* did not do the space justice. It was an alchemy lab. She wasn't sure why she was so surprised, Victor Ashdown was an alchemist after all, but it still caught her off guard. The quickly retreating light from a nearby window glinted on the edges of sparkling clean beakers and other glass containers. The various apparatus lining the walls and a central table made her think of her father.

Arhyen looked at Liliana, a perplexed twist to his mouth. "I don't know why, but I wasn't expecting to find a laboratory in his house."

She covered her mouth and let out a small laugh, amused they'd been thinking the same thought.

He glanced back into the space once more. "I'm assuming Ephraim already looked through this room, but we should check it again in the morning, just in case."

She nodded in agreement. "I might notice something that someone not versed in alchemy would have overlooked."

"Good thinking," he agreed, then yawned. "Now let's go lie down."

It struck her then that he hadn't eaten since they'd left the cafe that morning. Her guilt increased, but there was nothing she could do about it now. He seemed intent on lying down, perhaps out of energy from lack of food.

She followed somberly behind him as he strode back toward the first door. On top of her guilt she felt nervous, like she was breathing too quickly, but couldn't quite seem to control it. "Are you sure we're safe here?" she questioned breathily.

"We're not really safe anywhere," he replied absent-mindedly, glancing over his shoulder at her, "but here is as good a place as any, and hopefully no one will think to look for us in such an obvious location."

Unable to argue with his logic, she followed him into the dark bedroom. By the light of the newly risen moon she could see that the bed was large, fitting for two people, though she still had her reservations. She could always go back downstairs to keep watch once Arhyen was asleep. With that thought making her more comfortable, she sat crosslegged on the bed, smoothing her still damp dress around her knees. Arhyen flopped down onto the bed from the other side and laid his head on one of the pillows.

Silence ensued.

Suddenly realizing that she had nothing to talk about, she bit her lip and wracked her brain.

Arhyen saved her by speaking first. "Tell me about your life before we met."

She frowned. Why would he want to know about *that*? "It's not very interesting," she explained. "Plus, you should get some rest."

He shook his head against the pillow, drawing her gaze to him. "Consider it a bedtime story."

She sighed. Where to start? "I don't have very many memories from the time before father gave me a soul, or whatever it is he really gave me, so I suppose I'll start there," she began. "I vaguely remember when he had me inhale the compounds. I hadn't thought much of it, mainly because I never really thought much at all. I was just . . . blank."

"Mhhmm," he mumbled, his cheek against the pillow, prompting her to continue.

"The morning after that, everything changed," she went on. "Previously, I would sit in my room every night, because it's what my father ordered me to do, but I never slept. I didn't even have a bed, just a chair. I would just stare at the walls all night, until it was time to make father's breakfast. I did the same thing after inhaling the compounds, but it was different. After several hours, I stood up with this terrible feeling in the pit of my stomach. I was *afraid*. I looked around my room with the realization that I'd sat for eight hours in that little box every night of my life, after days of accomplishing *nothing*. I didn't even know how long I'd been alive. I still don't."

She began to grow more emotional as she spoke. The words felt like they were pouring out of her against her will. "I continued to suffer through that feeling every night for the next year. I was still an artificial construct. My purpose was to obey orders from my father, but I began to want *more*. I had never read any of his books before. I had no reason to. Yet I began to devour them whenever I had a free moment. I would sneak piles of them into my room after he'd gone to bed, and I would read all night. I learned all about history and technology, but what I truly enjoyed was fiction. I loved reading the books where young women would go out and have adventures. They would find their *purpose*, and sometimes they would even fall in love. I knew that I could never have that. I could never be like the characters in those books, and it crushed my heart every day until I finally just gave up. I shut off all of my newfound emotions. When I found my father's body, I felt nothing. I just went into that room and sat down, and did not move again until you showed up."

She glanced down at Arhyen, expecting him to be asleep, but his eyes were open and looking at her, reflecting the moonlight. He turned from his side and onto his back, then held out the arm nearest her.

She stared at it, not understanding the gesture.

"Come here," he said softly.

She did as he asked, curling up into the curve of his arm. It was a strange feeling, being that close to another body. It made her nervous, but at the same time, oddly comforted.

"You're not in that place anymore," he consoled. "You're more real than any of the characters in those books. You can have an adventure," he hesitated, "and you can find love, if that is your goal. And you know what?"

"What?" she asked weakly, squeezing her eyes shut to ward away tears.

"After you've had your adventure, and after you do anything else you want to do, it won't end like a book," he explained. "Your life will continue. You can make choices and find other things you want to do. I won't let anyone take that away from you."

She opened her eyes. Did he truly mean what he said? She turned to observe his face, but found only sincerity there. Her heart felt warm. It was the complete opposite of the horrible despair she'd come to know so well. "Why are you helping me?" she asked softly, not understanding why a man would do so much for a girl who wasn't even real.

He met her gaze steadily. "We all have our own cages to break free from. If I didn't help you, I wouldn't be deserving of ever getting help myself."

She smiled. "I will help you too, if I can."

He nodded and closed his eyes. "You already are," he whispered.

Still smiling, she slowly let her eyes fall shut, feeling calm for the first time in a very long time. Perhaps for the first time ever.

CHAPTER 14

Liliana's eyes slowly slid open. Gentle rays of early morning sunlight peeked through the window, casting shadows across the room. Arhyen remained asleep beside her, unmoving. At some point their clothes had finally dried, and a blanket had been placed over them, supposedly Arhyen's doing. He was a warm, comatose lump beside her. She took a moment to observe him, glad he'd finally gotten some rest. His dark eyelashes formed perfect half-circles on his scruffy face. Feeling suddenly embarrassed for observing him while he was unaware, she turned over to climb out of bed, then almost jumped out of her skin. There was someone leaning against the wall near the doorway, cloaked in shadows.

"It's about time," Ephraim's voice muttered tiredly.

The bed shifted as Arhyen sat bolt upright behind Liliana. She turned to see him rub his eyes blearily. "What the hell are you doing here?" he growled.

"Well I was beginning to think you both had perished," Ephraim explained caustically, pushing away from the wall with his elbows. "Clayton Blackwood reported a break-in at his estate. He claimed you were one of the perpetrators. I thought perhaps he had managed to find you before the Watch could."

Arhyen groaned, combing his fingers through his wayward hair. "Well that's *exactly* what I needed, another reason for the Watch to be on the lookout for me. Are they still searching?"

Ephraim nodded, then re-situated the gray coat that hung across his forearm. His hat hung limply from his hand.

"So how did you find us?" Arhyen asked, lowering his legs on the side opposite Liliana to climb out of bed. He quickly tugged on his boots and retrieved his satchel from the floor before standing.

Ephraim shrugged. "I simply made a list in my mind of the most likely locations to find you. It seemed logical that you would come somewhere where Clayton was unlikely to look. Also, I noticed that someone had stolen my key. Fortunately, I had a copy."

Liliana remained sitting on the bed as the men continued to banter. She was so embarrassed, she could hardly hear what they were saying. She had just slept the entire night in bed with a man, and now Ephraim knew about it. She'd had every intention of returning downstairs once Arhyen had fallen asleep, but she'd somehow fallen asleep as well. It seemed now that sleep was becoming habitual, it came more easily.

"Liliana?" Arhyen questioned curiously.

Startled by his voice, she realized he had moved around the bed and was now standing in front of her. She nervously smoothed her dress and hair, finding the latter snarled beyond rescue, then quickly stood, only to realize her shoes were missing. She looked down and found them resting beside the bed. Perhaps Arhyen had not gotten as much rest as she hoped.

"Yes?" she asked finally.

"I asked if you wanted to have a look at Ashdown's alchemy lab," he repeated with a soft smile.

She nodded quickly, then sat to don her shoes. Arhyen and Ephraim continued to speak of Clayton Blackwood while she laced them. Not hearing half the conversation, she quickly stood, then hurried out of the room ahead of the men, ignoring Ephraim's amused look.

The men followed behind her as she opened the door and rushed into the alchemy lab, lit by sunlight streaming through the window in the far wall. Sparing a nervous glance behind her, she instantly began her search, not wanting to invite any comments about the sleeping situation. She started with the bookcases, since that had worked before, perusing the various titles while dutifully ignoring Arhyen and Ephraim, until she realized neither of them were searching the room with her.

She paused her perusal and cast them a questioning look.

Ephraim shrugged. "I already searched this room top to bottom," he explained. "But I have little experience in alchemy, so you may find something I looked over."

Arhyen nodded his agreement, looking bedraggled with his wrinkled clothing and hair not easily tamed with fingers. "I probably know less about alchemy than Ephraim, so I'm a bit useless here."

Liliana turned back to the books with a sigh, uncomfortable with the pressure resting on her shoulders. Still, it would be nice if she did actually find something, in some way managing to contribute to the case.

Finding nothing remarkable about the books on the shelves, she turned toward the large workstation that dominated the center of the room. The station consisted of a rectangular table, topped with an alembic and other alchemical apparatus. Glass beakers and other containers were organized neatly on one end, most of them clean and empty.

She moved away from the table, toward another group of shelves, opposite the bookcases. There were many vials of different colored liquids, as well as jars that when opened, revealed different powders. She recognized most of the items from her years of aiding her father in his work. With the knowledge she'd gained during that time, she would probably even be able to create new compounds herself, though she had only ever tried simple formulas on her own.

She continued to search down the shelf until something caught her eye. It was bright green, and reminded her of the large gemstone they had found in the kitchen cabinet. She kneeled, smoothing her dress over her knees, ready to take a closer look. The men quietly approached behind her to see what she had found.

The green that had caught her eye was in fact a small shard of the same stone. It was suspended by a thin piece of twine that hung in a glass beaker half-filled with clear liquid. Where the stone met the liquid, what looked like copper had formed to partially engulf the gem.

Arhyen crouched beside her. "What's that liquid it's suspended in?"

Liliana took a moment to think. The copper seemed to be forming on its own, which could happen with the use of a copper chloride solution and an electric charge, though there was no source of power leading to the beaker.

"The only thing I can think of is copper chloride," she explained distantly, "but for such a reaction to take place, the liquid would need to have electric currents running through it. The process is called electroforming."

Arhyen stroked his stubbly chin in thought, gazing intently at the stone. "Is there any way to electrically charge an item so that it retains its charge even after the source of electricity has been removed?"

"It might be possible with certain metals or acids," she mused. "Many things conduct electricity, but it still has to come from somewhere. I don't see how the charge could be retained in copper chloride without a constant source of power, or within a gemstone."

Ephraim knelt on her other side, gazing closely at the suspended stone. "Unless it's not an ordinary gemstone," he offered. "I've never seen a stone with that particular hue. It's too bright to be an emerald. It almost seems to glow."

She considered that viewpoint for a moment, then held out her hand to Arhyen. "Give me the stone we found yesterday," she demanded.

Arhyen glanced at Ephraim, then sighed. Seeming quite unhappy, he removed the gemstone from his satchel and placed in her waiting palm.

Ephraim's eyebrow twitched at the sight of the large stone, but he did not speak.

Lifting the smaller stone out of the solution with her free hand, Liliana replaced it with the larger one, which barely fit into the beaker. On the surface of the liquid where it met the stone, minute crystals of copper began to form, much more quickly than they should have with a *normal* source of electricity. As the trio watched, the crystals slowly multiplied and crawled up the gem.

Liliana puckered her lips in thought. "The stone must have an electrical charge, though the crystals are forming more quickly than they should. You were right, Ephraim. The stone was likely made with alchemy, though I'm not sure how such a feat was accomplished. I've never heard of anything like it."

Arhyen stared at the stone, then turned his gaze to Ephraim. "Ephraim," he began, "I recall you saying something about our masked friend going on a little thieving spree. You claimed one of the items stolen was a gemstone. What type of stone was it?"

Ephraim raked his fingers through his neat blond hair as he stood. "The owner had been unable to determine what type of stone it was."

Arhyen rose, then helped Liliana to her feet. "It seems a strong coincidence that the masked man would lead us to Victor Ashdown, the owner of *this* odd stone," he gestured down at the beaker, "while that same man is said to have recently stolen a gemstone and other strange ingredients."

"He also stole a dead man's ashes," Ephraim replied blandly. "He may simply be a madman, without some complex plan."

"Maybe not," Liliana interrupted, a sudden thought hitting her. "Certain alchemical formulae call for biological components. Extracts from animal, or even human glands can be used. While the fire needed to create ash would destroy many of these compounds, some genetic material would remain."

The men looked at her as if she had just performed some amazing feat. She turned her gaze to the floor, suddenly embarrassed. She was only repeating what she'd read in her father's books.

"Do you know of any formulae that would require genetic components and electricity?" Arhyen asked hopefully.

She nodded somberly. She knew of one very important process that required some form of human genetic material, as well as electric currents to stimulate growth. "Both components are required to create an automaton," she explained.

The men fell silent. Liliana felt suddenly sick. Was the masked man creating automatons? And if so, would they be like her, with their own thoughts and feelings? He had her father's journal. If he was skilled in alchemy, it was possible.

"We need to look more into the stolen items," Ephraim stated suddenly. "With this new viewpoint, we may be able to gather more insight on the masked man's intent. Perhaps these clues will lead us to the reason why everyone wants Fairfax Breckenridge's journal, and also why they want Liliana."

Arhyen nodded in agreement. "After our encounter at Blackwood's estate yesterday, Liliana and I need to lay low, so the two of us should avoid Watch headquarters."

"Yes," Ephraim replied dryly, "especially if you'd like to avoid arrest."

Arhyen smiled somewhat apologetically, then continued. "We can visit some of the smaller alchemy shops and look for information on the stone."

Liliana glanced down at the stone in question. She *did* want to find out more about it, but going out in public seemed risky.

"It's settled then," Ephraim agreed before Liliana could interject.

Their individual missions now clear, Arhyen took a moment to retrieve the large, partially copper covered stone from the beaker. He shook off the extra moisture and returned it to his satchel. Liliana took one last glimpse around, then followed the men out of the room. They ascended the stairs in silence, then headed for the door.

Ephraim reached it first, then paused, his palm on handle. "I'll leave it to the two of you to find me," he explained. "It would be best for you to remain on the move. Don't stay in any one place for too long."

Arhyen nodded, then Ephraim opened the door, pausing to peek his head out to verify that no one lurked. He stepped outside, signaling all was clear. Arhyen retrieved Liliana's hat and coat from the nearby rack and helped her into them, then put his own hat on, before leading the way outside. He locked the door behind them, then they hurried down the few steps to the street. Without another word, Ephraim went one way, while Arhyen and Liliana went the other.

Arhyen's eyes darted around the street warily as they walked, flicking occasionally to Liliana. "Are you all right?" he questioned softly.

She nodded quickly, not sure whether she was actually alright. The street was still damp from the previous day's rain, and they had to weave back-and-forth to avoid large puddles. She hitched the collar of her coat up to obscure her face, feeling just as wary as Arhyen seemed to be.

"Where will we go first?" she questioned, speaking around the nervous lump in her throat. She was unsure whether her nerves were a result of the upcoming tasks, or if they had something to do with walking next to a man she'd just spent the night beside. Likely a mixture of both.

Arhyen continued to scan the buildings around them. "We will do exactly as I told Ephraim," he explained. "We will seek out alchemists to question about the gemstone, starting with Victor Ashdown's daughter."

Liliana stopped walking and turned toward him. "I don't believe that's what Ephraim intended for us to do."

Arhyen halted and smiled at her. "Of course not, but that doesn't mean that we shouldn't do it."

Liliana sighed, then followed him as he began walking again. With the short conversation, somehow the awkward tension had been lifted, though she still felt slightly nervous. She also felt uncomfortable with the notion of facing Victor Ashdown's daughter. Would she know who Liliana was? No women had ever visited her father's compound, but that did not mean that Victor had not appraised his daughter of his association with Fairfax Breckenridge. She supposed soon they would find out either way, though the encounter would likely only be one turn in the massive maze her father had created for her. She glanced at Arhyen again as they walked, sincerely hoping they weren't heading for a *dead* end.

❦

ARHYEN QUIETLY LOOKED OVER THE EXTERIOR OF Victor Ashdown's apothecary. It was unremarkable, except for the name, *Flowers of Antimony*. It was a strange name for an apothecary, considering such businesses usually went by the last name of the owner. *Bardsley's Apothecary, Erinson's Elixirs,* and so forth.

He glanced at Liliana, standing beside him, peering into the large glass windows of the storefront, her face partially shadowed by her hat. The walls inside the apothecary were lined with shelves filled with various bottles, as well as numerous displays in the center of the floor. Against the back wall was a long countertop where purchases could be made.

"Any idea what the flowers of antimony are?" he questioned.

"It's another name for antimony trioxide," she explained distantly, her gaze still on the storefront. "Depending on how you use it, it can take many forms. Heated with carbon, it can produce a type of metal. It can also be formed into a salt, and is often used in medicine. Reducing it with certain compounds can result in a highly toxic gas. I'm assuming that in naming his shop, Victor was referring to its medicinal properties."

Arhyen took a deep breath. "Let's hope so." With a final glance around the street to make sure they weren't being watched, they neared the shop and opened the door. He urged Liliana to walk inside before joining her.

Victor Ashdown's daughter stood behind the counter, grinding something furiously with a large stone mortar and pestle. Judging by Ashdown's photo in his police file, he'd been a full-blooded Englishman, which meant that his daughter received her looks from her mother. Her skin was a perfect dark brown, framed by black hair pulled away from her face in a tight bun. Her strong features spoke of Romani heritage. She wore a simple yellow dress, and did not seem to notice the two *customers* who had walked into her shop, though the door had an annoying bell attached to it.

Arhyen cleared his throat.

Without looking up, the woman stated, "I told you before, I know nothing more about my father than I already told the Watch."

Arhyen frowned, wishing he'd left on better terms with her on his previous visit.

Liliana approached the counter without a word. "I'm Fairfax Breckenridge's daughter," she stated, positioning herself directly in front of the woman, though the countertop divided them. "Does that mean anything to you?"

"Liliana-" Arhyen began, nervous that she'd divulged her identity to someone they couldn't trust. With so many dangerous people searching for her, even muttering her name behind closed doors was risky.

The woman finally looked up, sympathy clear in her expression, and Arhyen exhaled a sigh of relief. "The missing alchemist? I've heard rumors that he hasn't been seen for months."

Liliana nodded, removing the cap from her head to reveal her messy red locks, thrown hastily into snarled bun. "Yes, and I can understand why you don't want to answer any more questions, but I believe your father's disappearance has something to do with my father's death."

Arhyen cringed. Few knew that Fairfax Breckenridge was actually dead. The Watch had not released the information to the papers. It was best not to divulge unnecessary information. Still, Liliana seemed to be getting somewhere with Victor's daughter, so he stood back and remained silent.

"Death?" the woman questioned nervously, her full lips forming into a frown.

Liliana nodded again. "Yes, he was murdered," she explained, "and I'm trying to find out why. My name is Liliana, by the way," she added conversationally.

"I'm Chirani," the woman introduced, "and I'm sorry about your father, but I don't understand what his death could have to do with my father's disappearance."

"Our fathers were friends," Liliana explained. "I met Victor Ashdown on several occasions, though I was introduced to him by a different name."

Chirani shook her head. "That's not possible. I'm sure if my father had known the great Fairfax Breckenridge, he would have told me."

Sensing his opportunity, Arhyen stepped forward, retrieving the large green stone from his satchel as he went. He held the stone up. "Do you recognize this?"

Chirani's dark eyes widened. "Where did you get that?" she gasped.

"Please," Liliana pleaded. "Can you tell us what this is?"

Chirani held out her hand for the stone. Arhyen placed

it reluctantly in her palm, hoping she would not try to keep it. Chirani glanced one more time at Liliana's sad face, then sighed. "This was a creation of my father's. He'd yet to announce it to the world, so he kept it well-hidden, worried that someone would steal his idea."

"What does it do?" Liliana pressed.

"It generates electricity," Chirani explained.

"Why did your father create it?" Liliana asked a little too quickly.

Chirani's eyes narrowed in suspicion, but she answered, "Really, I have no idea. Why *wouldn't* someone want to create an object that can generate electricity on its own. If I had any idea how it was made, I would already be selling them in my shop."

Arhyen sighed. This woman truly didn't know any more than they did. In fact, she knew even less.

Chirani leaned forward across the countertop with the stone still in her palm, though her gaze was intent on Liliana. "Please," she whispered. "I can tell you know something about my father that you're not letting on. I've answered your questions, now *please* tell me what you know."

Arhyen glanced at Liliana as she bit her lip. He had a feeling she was about to spill everything. Not only was it a good practice to keep information to yourself, but if Chirani knew certain things, it might put her in danger.

Before he could cut in, Liliana answered, "If I find anything out about your father, I swear to you that you'll be the first person I tell."

He heaved another sigh of relief. He really needed to give Liliana more credit.

Chirani looked down at the stone in her hand, then extended it to Liliana. "If this will somehow aid in your search for information, please keep it. I have several others stashed away until I can find the time to unravel how they work."

Liliana took the stone in her gloved hand, then offered it to Arhyen, who Chirani turned to with a frown. Not making eye contact, he dropped the stone into his satchel, though Chirani continued to stare.

Arhyen forced his gaze upward, meeting her stare.

Having gained his full attention, she stated, "I don't know what your part in all of this is, but I trust you'll keep her safe?" She nodded at Liliana. "It can be difficult for a young woman to lose her father, to be left to make her own way in the world. I should know."

He smiled genuinely. "It seems *she's* the one keeping *me* safe half the time, but still, I'll do my best."

Chirani nodded, satisfied. "Now if you'll excuse me, I have several orders I need to finish."

They said their goodbyes and departed. Liliana seemed somehow satisfied, but Arhyen couldn't help but be disappointed at the lack of new information. They'd verified the stone's purpose, but little else, and he had no idea where to go from there. He knew further investigation into Clayton Blackwood was the logical next step, but there was no way he was bringing Liliana near that man again. It was too risky. They would simply have to wait for Ephraim to obtain further information on the stolen items.

His mind made up, he guided Liliana away from the main street. They would lay low until it was time to find Ephraim, then they'd proceed cautiously. As the self-proclaimed greatest thief in London, caution really wasn't his style, but he'd found Liliana had changed him . . . in more ways than one.

CHAPTER 15

L iliana thought over everything Chirani had said as she and Arhyen made their way down the gloomy, deserted street. It wasn't much, really. They were no closer to finding answers. She wished she'd had the courage to show Chirani the recreated journal. Perhaps she might have recognized the formulae. She might have even been able to *make* them. Really, Liliana probably could have created the formulae in her father's journal herself, but there was no saying if they would actually turn out correctly. She feared what might happen if they decided to test the unknown formulae, and she had made them wrong.

Her thoughts were cut off as several forms stepped into view on the street ahead of them. They'd stepped out of the nearest intersection, leaving Liliana and Arhyen bordered by tall buildings and fences on either side. She turned quickly, only to find three more men standing in the street behind them, blocking any chance of retreat. Though the men did not have white strips of fabric tied around their arms like the previous group they'd encountered, it was obvious they meant them harm. There was no mistaking the way they'd positioned themselves to block the street in either direction. She and Arhyen were effectively trapped, unless they were able to somehow scale the nearby wire fence. There was a chance she might manage it, but would have trouble with the razor wire spiraled around the top, and she wouldn't leave Arhyen behind regardless. She considered screaming for help, but they were on the outskirts of the industrial district. The buildings surrounding them appeared to be vacant warehouses, so no help would likely be found from anyone dwelling within.

The men in front of them began to approach. Arhyen wrapped an arm around her waist, pulling her close as the footsteps of the other men echoed behind them, closing in. They backed toward the tall brick building opposite the fence, angling so their backs would not be to any of the men. Liliana darted her gaze left and right to the sneering faces slowly surrounding them. She expected them to attack at any moment, but once they'd closed in, no one moved.

A moment later, she found out why. The sound of high-heeled boots echoed on the cobblestones, then Viola walked into view around the street corner. Her black coat and dress contrasted sharply with her pale skin and rouged lips. She was taller than Liliana had originally envisioned, since she'd only seen the woman sitting down during their one meeting. Her second impression of her was not any more favorable than the first. She moved to stand near her small army of men, safely out of reach.

"I didn't think we'd find you so easily," Viola purred, placing a hand possessively on one of the men's arms while she eyed Liliana. "Clayton will be furious that I found you first."

"Does he know that you had his men killed?" Arhyen asked evenly.

Liliana glanced up at Arhyen, then back to Viola. Was he lying? Ephraim had made it clear they didn't know *who* had killed Clayton Blackwood's men, but that the masked man was a suspect.

Viola laughed, then walked past the waiting men, putting herself closer to Liliana and Arhyen. "He'll know when I'm ready to tell him," she explained.

Liliana was doing her best to remain calm. She wasn't worried about her own safety, but if these people managed to kidnap her, she feared what might happen to Arhyen. She had little doubt that the men had nothing nice planned for either of them.

As if sensing her thoughts, Arhyen glanced down at her. "When you get the chance," he whispered, "*run*."

She shook her head, wondering why he continued to give her those same orders when she never obeyed. "I won't leave you."

Viola cackled. "How cute, the automaton seems to think that it's a real person. Arhyen, tell the girl the truth. She's little more than a bargaining chip to you."

"On the contrary," he replied smoothly, still holding Liliana close, "she's my apprentice. There's nothing more valuable than a student that's willing to learn."

Viola snorted. "Apprentice to what? Petty thievery and amateur card playing?"

Arhyen laughed, startling Liliana. "I seem to recall you losing your fair share of chips the other night, many of them to *her*." He gave Liliana's waist a tight squeeze.

Viola's red lips curved downward into a frown. "Enough of this," she snapped. "Grab them," she instructed her men. "Leave the girl alive. Kill the man if you must."

Almost too quick for Liliana's eyes to follow, Arhyen pulled away from her and produced a knife from his sleeve. With a perfectly timed throw, he flung it at the nearest man. It hit the center of the man's throat with a sickening *thwack*. Blood spewed forth and he fell to his knees, gurgling and gasping for breath.

Momentarily shocked, Liliana could not bring herself to move as chaos ensued around her. She heard the minute tinkling sound of a small amount of glass breaking, then thick gray smoke billowed around them. She squinted her eyes, unable to see farther than her outstretched hand.

"Run!" Arhyen rasped, but Liliana could not bring herself to move. She had to help in some way, but how?

She was about to step forward, then there was another meaty *thunk* just to her left. A man rolled into view on the ground at her feet, clutching at a knife in his gut as his gray shirt darkened with blood. Alarmed by the man's dying presence, she squinted her eyes through the smoke and forced herself to step forward. Someone grabbed her arm and she screamed, then reflexively lashed out. Her fist slammed into her attacker's throat. Gasping for air, he reared away in surprise, loosing his grip on her arm.

She had no time to be relieved. Another man appeared in the rapidly dissipating smoke and made a grab for her. She flung her arm out and backhanded him in the face. She was stronger than a normal girl of her size, and it seemed to be catching the men off guard. Her new attacker reeled backward, but another one was there to instantly take his place. Still, she managed to elude any who tried to grab her, and soon found her back against the wall as three of the men approached. She could not see Arhyen, but more smoke had fogged the street to her left, and sounds of struggle emanated from within. She tore her attention away from the smoke and prepared to fight her new attackers. They were all large men. If they managed to grab her together, it would all be over.

She lifted her fists, wishing she actually knew how to

throw a proper punch, then Viola's voice cut through the madness.

"Your *partner*," she stated, "is about to die. Come with us willingly, and we will spare him."

Liliana looked past the approaching men to see that what Viola had said was true. The smoke had cleared away enough to reveal Arhyen, held immobile with a knife to his throat. The man behind him holding the knife, a lanky character with a large scar running across his cheek, looked to Viola for further orders. Two extra men held either of Arhyen's arms. They glanced around the street, as if worried someone else might approach. Even if someone did, it wouldn't matter. More men had crept forth from the shadows of the intersections. Arhyen had no chance of escape. Liliana held back tears, noticing his left sleeve was soaked in blood. The crimson liquid ran down his hand to drip onto the cobblestones.

Making her decision instantly, Liliana tore her gaze from Arhyen and nodded to Viola.

"*No*," Arhyen gasped, despite the blade at his throat. "Even if you go with her, they'll kill me anyways. Run while you can."

Liliana glanced back to Viola.

"I give you my word that he will not be harmed," Viola ensured. "His death is useless to me. You're the one I want."

"Don't-" Arhyen began. The lanky man with the blade flexed his arm, adding pressure to cut off his words.

Liliana scowled at him.

"I'll go with you," she agreed, feeling ill at the sight of the blade against Arhyen's throat. "Just don't hurt him. If I find out that you've harmed him, I will do everything it takes to destroy your plans. But," she paused, knowing she shouldn't make the deal she was about to offer, yet knowing she had no choice, "as long as you provide me with proof that he's alive, I will cooperate with you in any way that you ask."

Viola chuckled. "Well that was easy."

"No!" Arhyen shouted, but was once again cut off by the knife.

Ignoring Arhyen, Viola approached. She flicked her hand absentmindedly at the three men who still cornered Liliana, and as one they backed away. Viola moved to stand directly in front of her, putting her back to Arhyen and everyone else. Liliana had to crane her neck upward to meet her cool gaze.

Viola smiled. "My men will release him as soon as you and I have moved to a secure location."

Liliana nodded and took a step forward, just as Viola turned to lead the way. Hesitating, she glanced back at Arhyen, still held captive by the thugs.

"Liliana," he whispered, but could say no more. Blood welled at his throat to trickle down onto his collar.

Feeling sick to her stomach, Liliana turned away and followed Viola. The men who had cornered her followed closely behind. *Please let him be okay*, she thought. All of her life, her father had instructed her that automatons were never supposed to harm humans. Automatons were not real people, and therefore were not allowed to defend themselves. Though she still found the idea of harming others troubling, for Arhyen, she would fight. If Viola went back on her word, Liliana would tear the woman limb from limb, and would then lay waste to any who had harmed him.

ARHYEN WATCHED HELPLESSLY AS LILIANA WAS LED AWAY. Viola had tricked her. There was no way he was getting out of the situation alive. The blade at his throat remained as the women and their escorts disappeared down the street. He needed to save her, but first he had to survive.

Blood continued to trickle forth from the blade's pressure at his throat, but the pain was a dull echo to what he was feeling in his arm. One of the men had stabbed him in the shoulder, though he'd been aiming for Arhyen's heart. It was only because he'd moved to throw a dagger into someone about to attack Liliana that he'd evaded the killing blow.

"Do you really plan to murder me in broad daylight?" he questioned around the pain.

"No," the man holding the blade to his throat answered. "We have other plans for you. It's time to go meet your friend."

The blade fell away and Arhyen struggled, but the two extra men still held his arms, and more were waiting should he break free. One of the men holding him removed the satchel from his shoulders, handing it to one of the other thugs before thoroughly searching Arhyen for weapons. Arhyen did his best to keep his eyes off the satchel, where the recreated journal rested. He didn't want anyone thinking anything of import could be found within the bag. He must have succeeded, because no one bothered to search through it, though they could always do so later. Having removed all but one of his daggers, they forced him down the street, in the opposite direction of where Liliana had gone. A few men stayed behind to dispose of the bodies. The Watch was really failing when bodies could be disposed of in daylight, but they *were* in an area rarely patrolled. Viola had chosen the location for her ambush wisely, and Arhyen had led Liliana right into her trap. The jab of a fist into his back signaled he should move faster.

The man who'd held the blade to his throat caught his

eye. "Don't worry," he comforted in a not at all comforting way. "We don't have to go far."

Glaring at the man, he briefly considered his remaining dagger, concealed within a special pocket in his boot. Unfortunately, now was not the time to use it. One weapon would not help him much against so many opponents. He walked slowly, hoping an opportunity to escape would present itself. He quietly observed the buildings around their route, searching for anything that might be of use. Though no escape plans came to him, he did become quite sure of where they were going. He recognized the nearby buildings and alleyways. This was the same route he had taken the night he was supposed to meet Viola. They were heading right for one of her steel manufacturing plants.

Knowing he was running out of time, he began to struggle anew, but it was no use. There was no way he was getting himself out of this predicament, unless someone came along to rescue him. Not likely, since new, larger plants were being used for most of London's manufacturing these days. As the industry grew, there was always need for bigger and better things. Eventually he found himself in front of the large warehouse doors of the steel plant.

Arhyen stared up at the double doors, hoping his captors had perhaps forgotten their keys, then the doors seemed to open of their own volition. The men holding him shoved him forward into the building. Once they were all inside, the doors swung shut behind them, revealing an extra thug who'd been waiting inside the building to let them in.

The men fanned out, then finally let go of him, but only to shove him hard enough that he fell to his knees. He glanced around the dark building. Twenty paces ahead of him stood a large, metal cylinder, backed by several other vessels. A steel staircase led up to the cylinder, rimmed with storage barrels. The floor was littered with various discarded gears and chunks of iron ore. Apparently the plant had been out of commission for some time, just like the other manufacturers surrounding it. Gaining nothing from his surroundings, he pushed himself to standing and glared at the waiting men, attempting to calculate his odds with his single dagger, though realistically he knew he stood no chance. Viola could be doing terrible things to Liliana right that moment, and it was all his fault. He'd failed her.

His shoulders hunched against his will, his body giving in to the pain of his wound and the humiliation of losing. Feeling utterly defeated, he barely fought as more of the men grabbed him, then dragged him across the floor. He half walked as they carried him up the set of steel stairs, toward the nearest metal cylinder. His mind blankly registered a panel of electrical switches near the stairs, and two rows of windows high up in the walls, letting in a small amount of light. Reaching the top of the steps, then men lifted him into the air and tossed him like a rag doll into the cylinder. He landed hard on his side at the bottom of the container, roughly five yards deep. Pain seared through his hip and arm. Even the puncture wound on his shoulder stung like hell. He sucked in a breath to recover, then rolled onto his back just in time to see the men who had thrown him in disappear into the shadows above the cylinder. Their footsteps clanged down the metal stairs, obscuring their hushed conversation. Next he heard the warehouse doors as they screeched open, then shut with a loud *bang*. Then there was only silence.

"It's about time you got here," a voice said.

Still wracked with pain, he forced himself to sit up. Ephraim sat to his left with his back against the wall of the cylinder. He was barely visible in the shadows of the large container, but Arhyen would recognize his dry sarcasm anywhere.

Pushing himself up on his feet, Arhyen glanced around at their enclosure, seeing no footholds or other way out. Even if one of the men boosted the other one up, they would not be able to reach the lip of the container.

"How long have you been here?" Arhyen questioned. He began to pace around the space, counting his steps out of habit. He held a hand over his shoulder wound, though the bleeding had fortunately slowed. No major arteries had been severed.

Ephraim sighed tiredly. "I was abducted before I even made it back to the station. They took me by surprise, as I surely would have thwarted them otherwise."

"Surely," Arhyen muttered caustically.

He halted his pacing. The container was fifteen paces across in any direction, not that the information helped him. He looked up, wracking his brain for some other way to escape. Perhaps they could take off all their clothes to form a rope . . . of course, how they'd attach it somewhere outside of the cylinder was beyond him.

"Where's Liliana?" Ephraim inquired calmly

Arhyen simply shook his head, staring up at the rim of the container, unable to speak it out loud. It was all his fault. He *had* to get out of there.

He turned in time to see Ephraim frown. "I've deduced that this container is a crucible," he explained, glancing at the surrounding wall, "which means that at some point we are probably going to be melted along with a bunch of metal ore."

"Well that's comforting," Arhyen quipped, starting his pacing anew.

"At least you know you'll probably die before her."

He tried to find comfort in that fact, but found himself unable to give up so easily. He continued to pace.

"Perhaps some vagrants will arrive to rest for the evening before Viola's men return," Ephraim offered. When Arhyen didn't respond, Ephraim sighed. "At least come here and let me have a look at that wound." He stood with a huff.

Arhyen stopped his pacing and nodded, then approached Ephraim. Quickly deducing the source of the blood without removing Arhyen's shirt, Ephraim unwound the ascot tie from his neck and deftly secured it around Arhyen's shoulder, anchoring it beneath his armpit.

Finished, he nodded. "If we manage to survive, you'll want to have that looked at by a professional."

Arhyen prepared a snide remark, but froze at the sound of the warehouse door opening with a screech and then shutting. He and Ephraim kept silent, listening to several pairs of footsteps creeping across the warehouse. One set seemed to ascend the steel stairway. Apparently, whoever else was there remained waiting at the base. Arhyen could barely breathe in anticipation. His heart pounded hard as he held his eyes fast at the top of the cylinder. A man's face appeared, peeking over the cylinder's top edge, his blue eyes sparkling in the dim light behind gold-rimmed glasses.

"What are *you* doing here?" Arhyen asked tiredly.

"I've been itching to make you pay for the deaths of my men," Clayton said, his eyes intent on Arhyen. "Now that we have the girl, I'm sure that I'll be able to obtain the journal without your help."

Arhyen glared up into Clayton's smiling face. Viola's men had taken his satchel, so they already had the recreated journal, but he wasn't going to point that out now. "Has Viola told you she's the one that killed your men and left them on your doorstep?" he asked instead.

Clayton snorted. "You won't fool me that easily." Though he outwardly projected confidence, his hand shook as he smoothed it over his blond hair. Had he already suspected Viola's duplicity?

Arhyen laughed bitterly. Any man who would trust a woman like Viola was a fool. "You really think I'm capable of killing that many men?" he countered. "What about how their mutilated bodies appeared outside your gate with no one noticing their arrival? I'm only one man."

"You had the help of your *detective* friend," Clayton sneered.

"Oh yes, blame the detective," Ephraim muttered. He'd resumed his seat against the cylinder's wall, showing little interest in Clayton's arrival.

"Say Viola did kill my men," Clayton mused, "what would you hope to gain by sharing that information with me? You're still about to die."

"I'm assuming you know what she intends to do with Liliana?" Arhyen pressed, fishing for information. What he would do with that information from within the cylinder he did not know, but it couldn't hurt.

Clayton snorted. "The automaton? Of course I know. Viola and I have been working together a long time. As two of the top business owners in the city, we have worked together to build an empire. Now that we have the automaton, and will soon have the journal, no one, not even the *LN*, will stand in our way."

So they weren't really part of the mysterious London Network, Arhyen mused. Not that the information would do him any good now. He'd probably die without ever truly knowing what the *LN* was.

Clayton smiled down at Arhyen's thoughtful expression. "That's enough talk. Time to die."

"Clayton wait," Arhyen begged. "Liliana doesn't know

where the journal is. I hid it, and I'm the only one who knows how to find it. If I die, any hope of getting those formulae dies with me."

"You're lying," Clayton accused, then seemed to actually think about what Arhyen had said. "But just in case, I will verify this information with the lovely little automaton before I kill you. I'll be sure to give her your regards."

"Clayton!" Arhyen shouted as the man turned to go. Curse it all, he'd only made things worse. Now the psychopath would be *questioning* Liliana in addition to whatever Viola had planned.

Unbearably frustrated with himself, Arhyen listened for Clayton's descending footfalls, but instead heard several sets coming up the stairs. Clayton's waiting men?

"What are you-" Clayton began, but his words were cut off. A moment later, he came sailing over the edge of the cylinder, landing in a heap right next to Arhyen. Two thugs peered over the rim.

Arhyen sneered at the men, then stared down at Clayton cooly. "I *tried* to tell you. Viola has been planning to cross you from the start."

Arhyen glanced upward to see the two nameless thugs retreat.

Clayton groaned again, but seemed unable to stand.

Footsteps thundered down the steel staircase, then the screech of metal components being moved echoed through the warehouse. Next, a long metal chute appeared at the top edge of the cylinder. The machinery groaned, and chunks of iron ore began to rain down upon them. Arhyen hurried to the opposite side of the cylinder next to where Ephraim still sat to avoid being pelleted. The next logical step in the process was for the blast furnace to be activated, and at that point, they would all be toast.

Clayton slowly struggled to sit up beneath the deluge of

ore. He scooted across the floor of the cylinder, searching for something. Catching on, Ephraim rose to his feet to avoid the encroaching sea of ore, then retrieved Clayton's gold-rimmed glasses just before they would have been buried. Ephraim handed them to Clayton as he finally stumbled to his feet. Clayton put them on, though they were badly bent, and one lens was cracked.

"We have to get out of here," he stated, his eyes shifting back and forth between Arhyen and Ephraim as the mountain of ore grew.

"There are three of us now," Ephraim observed calmly. *How was the man always so damn calm?* "Someone will need to get down on their hands and knees, then the next man can stand atop him. With the added height, we should be able to boost the third man out. If we can't quite reach, we'll try piling up the ore for extra height."

"Then the first man out can fight the ruffians, then quickly save the other two," Arhyen finished, sarcasm clear in his voice. "But as far as plans go, it's the only one." He turned to Clayton. "I think you know who's going to be on the bottom."

Clayton glared. The ore was piling up around their ankles. If they waited long enough, perhaps they could simply stand on top of the ore and climb out together, but Arhyen had a feeling the blast furnace would fire long before that became a possibility.

He looked back to Clayton. "Down you go," he ordered.

The men manning the smelter were oddly quiet up above, but Arhyen had no time to dwell upon it.

Grumbling to himself, Clayton got down on his knees in the loose rocks of ore. Ephraim seemed almost gleeful as he stood on the well-known criminal's back. He leaned against the wall of the cylinder to stabilize himself, then laced his hands together to provide a foothold for Arhyen. Not taking time to consider what might await him above, Arhyen stepped onto Ephraim's waiting hands and pushed upward with all his might. His fingers found the edge of the cylinder, but they still didn't have enough height. Arhyen had sorely underestimated the depth of the container, as he was barely able to curve his fingertips around the lip. As it stood, he'd never be able to pull himself up.

Just when he was about to give up and drop back down, a black-gloved hand grabbed his wrist and hauled him upward. Whoever had grabbed him was incredibly strong, and within seconds he was out of the cylinder, sprawled across the upper landing of the steel staircase, panting with shock and exertion. He gazed up at the man standing over him, taking in his solid black clothing, and smooth, porcelain mask.

"*You*," he breathed. He glanced behind him to see the two thugs lying bloody and broken at the bottom of the stairs.

The masked man had Arhyen's satchel slung across his shoulders. Had he intercepted the men on their way back to Viola? If he'd searched the satchel, he'd know about the recreated journal. Would he now kill Arhyen too? Before he could speak, the man lifted the satchel and held it out to him. He took it gingerly, still staring at the man in disbelief.

"The thugs who brought me here?" Arhyen questioned, requiring affirmation.

"Dead," the man said evenly.

Arhyen's eyes widened in surprise. For some reason he had built up the persona in his head that the masked man could not, or would not, speak. When he'd asked the question, he hadn't really expected an answer.

"Still down here!" Ephraim called from within the cylinder.

Arhyen cast a wary glance at the masked man, then rose to

his feet and hurried down the steel stairway. He should have moved sooner, but he'd been too dumbfounded to act. The ore was still pouring into the cylinder, and the blast furnace could activate any second. He needed a rope or something else to lower down to Ephraim. He glanced around as the masked man stood calmly at the top of the stairs. He pointed to a lever on the wall next to Arhyen. The shut off switch? Hoping this all wasn't some horrible trick, he reached out and pulled it downward. The ore chute shut off, and the room fell silent.

His hand still on the lever, he stared up at the masked man.

"*Still* down here!" Ephraim called out again.

Arhyen jumped into motion, while the masked man continued to wait silently. He hurried away from the lever, and searched the lower portion of the room. He peeked inside a few barrels, finding nothing of use, but eventually found a folded stack of canvas bags. Three tied together should do the trick. His hands moving quickly, he assembled the makeshift rope, then hurried back up the stairs.

He hesitated at the top, wary of moving too close to the masked man, but he *had* just saved everyone's lives, and Ephraim would probably kill Arhyen himself if he dallied any longer. As the masked man watched on, Arhyen tied off one end of the makeshift rope on the railing of the staircase, then lowered the other end into the cylinder. He would be useless tugging anyone up with his injured shoulder, so hopefully they were both in good enough condition to climb. Well, hopefully Ephraim was, at least.

Down in the cylinder, Ephraim glared at Clayton until he backed away, then hopped up to catch the end of the rope. He effortlessly climbed up, requiring no aid to pull himself over the lip of the cylinder. Clayton's climb was slightly less graceful, and Arhyen finally had to grab under

Clayton's shoulder with his good arm to haul him out. It was tempting to just let him fall back in, but he needed to find out where Liliana was, so he resisted. Clayton hunched against the outside of the cylinder, exhausted and panting, obviously not an immediate threat.

Standing beside Arhyen, Ephraim dusted off his gray trousers, then cast his gaze on the masked man, who stood silently, as if waiting for something.

"Is this the man who stole the journal?" Ephraim questioned calmly.

Arhyen nodded, warily eyeing the man before them.

"*Stole?*" Clayton panted. He'd moved a few paces to crouch as far away from everyone as possible, while still remaining on the upper landing. "You mean you don't even *have* the journal?"

It was amusing to see the normally immaculate man covered in black stains, his hair a total mess, and his broken glasses askew, but there was no time for Arhyen to enjoy the moment. "Yes, it was stolen," he answered. "Now tell me where Viola took Liliana."

Clayton stood up straight, though he seemed to be favoring his left leg. "And lose the one piece of leverage I have left?" He glanced nervously at the masked man. "I don't think so."

Faster than Arhyen could blink, the masked man whipped out a long, narrow blade, darted forward, then shoved it through Clayton's abdomen, up underneath his ribcage toward his heart. Finding his target, the man expertly withdrew the blade. Clayton stumbled on his feet for a moment, then fell at Arhyen's feet, dead.

Arhyen took a step back, then turned wide eyes up to the masked man. "Why?" he croaked.

"I know where the girl is being kept," the man replied

calmly in a cultured voice, slightly muffled by his mask. "It was not necessary to keep Blackwood alive."

Arhyen spread his arms wide. "No, I mean *why*? Why all of this? Why lead me to Victor Ashdown? Why frame me for murder? Why save us now?"

"We haven't much time if you want to save Liliana," the man said cooly.

Shit. As much as Arhyen wanted answers, the man had him there. "Lead the way," he demanded, despite the bloody blade hanging threateningly in the masked man's grip.

Flicking the blood from the blade, the man resheathed it somewhere within his coat, then glided past Arhyen and Ephraim down the stairs toward the warehouse's double doors. He effortlessly pushed the doors open, revealing darkness and heavy rain, then stepped outside. Arhyen glanced down at Clayton's body, then met Ephraim's gaze. Ephraim nodded, and both men hurried down the stairs and out into the night, prepared to follow the masked murderer wherever he might lead them.

CHAPTER 16

Liliana glanced around the room as much as her neck would allow. The walls and floor had all been painted white, and shelves of what looked like medical equipment lined the edges of the room. She was strapped down on a padded table, with canvas strips not only wrapped around her wrists and ankles, but at intervals down her entire body, holding her entirely immobile. She'd been forced to change into a white nightshift, and her dress had been disposed of.

She tried to shift uncomfortably, but to no avail. She'd been lying there for what felt like hours, with no explanation. Her limbs ached, and her hands felt numb from circulation loss. She stared at the bare, overhead bulb lighting the room. Though she did not suffer from the cold as much as humans, she felt it right then.

Viola had left her alone shortly after she'd been placed in the room, with no assurances about Arhyen's safety. She was beginning to realize she'd been a fool to cooperate and let Viola not only kidnap her, but strap her down. Perhaps she could have saved Arhyen some other way. She struggled against her bonds for the hundredth time, thinking about Arhyen. Was he even still alive? It was too late for regrets now. It was too late for *anything*. Even if Arhyen somehow managed to escape Viola's men, there was no way he'd find her now.

Though the building she'd willingly entered had seemed unremarkable from the outside, inside, it was like one of the fictional futuristic novels Liliana had read while she still lived with her father. There had been different pieces of machinery that she could identify, like an autoclave for sterilizing equipment and centrifuge for separating liquids, as well as tools more specific to alchemy and metallurgy. In addition to the myriad of scientific devices, there had been large, liquid-filled glass tubes, some containing what looked like tiny humans, and others filled with individual body parts or organs. She hadn't had time to look at them closely, but knew the brief glimpses she'd had would give her nightmares for a long time to come. If she lived for a long time to come. Naturally, the research within the building was well-guarded. Even if she managed to escape her bonds, she'd have no chance of sneaking past the pistol-wielding guards.

Her mind flashed again on the liquid-filled tubes. Would she end up in one herself? A few weeks ago, she might not have really cared. Death had seemed a viable option when she was stranded in the darkness with her father's corpse. Things had changed since then. She'd been offered a true taste of life, and she was loath to let it go so quickly. She struggled against her bonds once more, but it was no use. There would be no escape.

She jumped as the door to the room opened, and high-heeled boots sounded on the bare concrete floor. Seconds later, Viola came to hover over her. She now wore a thin white coat over her black apparel, and silver spectacles perched on the tip of her narrow nose. "Forgive me for leaving you alone for so long," she apologized, her red lips curving into a smile that belied her kind words. "I had to ensure that all my loose ends were tied up. As things stand now, no one will ever be able to find you. At least, not until I'm done with you."

It was just as Liliana had thought. No one was coming for her. "What about Arhyen?" she pleaded. "You swore you would not harm him."

"Did I?" Viola questioned sarcastically. "My memory is terrible, I must have forgotten."

Tears began to drip down Liliana's face. Her fists flexed with rage. If only she could get her hands around Viola's throat.

Viola moved a bare hand to wipe away Liliana's tears. "She cries," she mocked. "I must admit, Fairfax did a brilliant job at simulating emotions. You almost seem *real.*" She moved away briefly, then her footsteps were accompanied by the sound of a rickety metal table being wheeled over. He face came back into view, an evil gleam in her dark eyes.

Liliana glared at her, forcing her tears to abate. "What are you talking about? What do you mean, *simulating emotions?*"

"Why, that's the entire reason everyone has been searching for you," Viola explained, fiddling with something on the table out of Liliana's sight. "Your father managed not only to create synthetic rage, sadness, and joy. He managed to create synthetic love. He used Victor Ashdown's serum to administer them to you. You were his experiment, nothing more."

"I don't know what you're talking about," she croaked, fresh tears straining her voice. All she could think about was Arhyen. Had Viola broken her promise and harmed him? Was her entire sacrifice for nothing?

"Imagine how powerful bottled emotions could be, in the right hands," Viola mused. She turned away from Liliana, and paced around the room, leaving the metal table behind. "They could be used to rule nations. Imagine administering bottled rage to your enemies, forcing them to kill each other. Imagine what people would pay for bottled joy. It would put any other drug to shame. Now, imagine that I control all these things. Why, I could rule the world."

Liliana continued to cry. "Are you the one who killed my father?"

Viola snorted. "No, in fact, I wasn't even aware that he was dead, though I'm not surprised. I only knew that he had not been seen for quite some time. Around the time he disappeared, rumors began to circulate of what he had created. Anyone with a brain wanted to get their hands on those formulae, and anyone with the correct information knew that Victor Ashdown knew how to do that."

"Victor Ashdown?" she questioned weakly. After all that had happened, she'd almost forgotten about him. She recalled the note from her father in Victor's book. Victor had known he was going to die, and knew that Fairfax would eventually be next. That meant the rumors about Fairfax's formulae had begun to circulate before her father's death, but she saw no point in voicing that to Viola. Still, she wondered who had started all of this. Who had leaked her father's research, and why?

"But you still don't have the journal," Liliana observed. "You still don't have your hands on the formulae that you need. So why take me?"

Viola grinned and lifted a shiny silver scalpel into her hand from the nearby table. Liliana struggled, craning her neck to see what Viola was doing. She lifted the scalpel to Liliana's neck and dragged it across her skin. After the initial sting, Liliana felt her blood slowly dripping down her skin in a warm line.

"You're right," Viola answered, twirling the scalpel in her fingers. "I am yet to obtain the journal, but I have *you*. Your blood contains those very formulae. All I need to do is extract it and refine it." She stroked her bare finger down Liliana's bleeding neck, then held the bloody appendage up to her lips. Her tongue flicked out, tasting the blood.

"You're mad," Liliana gasped.

"We'll see," Viola replied, setting the scalpel back on the tray. Then she lifted an empty syringe. "Once I have your blood, no one will dare call me mad. I'll be as powerful as the Queen. More so, if I have my way."

Liliana struggled against her bonds, unable to take her gaze off the shiny silver needle at the end of the syringe. She didn't want to die here. "What did you mean about my father creating love?" she blurted, grasping at the first thought that came to her. She needed to keep Viola talking to buy time. Time for what, she was not sure.

Viola sneered. "I have on high authority that Fairfax Breckenridge created four special formulae. They simulate the chemical reactions that occur in the brain during different emotions. He created one for happiness, one for sadness, one for *rage*," her mouth placed emphasis on the word, as if she very much enjoyed using it, "and one for love," she finished. "They are of course, not true emotions, only chemical reactions to simulate emotions. Though why their components continue to affect you long after the initial administration, I am not sure. I'm no alchemist."

Liliana made no effort to hide her confusion. Viola had said nothing about manufacturing *fear*, yet that was exactly what she was feeling. Had her father created more than just the four formulae, or had she perhaps developed other emotions after receiving the first few? More confusing still, was the fact that her emotions were in direct correlation with events. They came and went. Had her father conditioned her to feel emotions at the correct times? She wasn't sure.

While she was deep in thought, Viola had once again lifted the syringe. Without warning, she jammed it into Liliana's arm.

All of her previous thoughts rushing away, she screamed.

⚜

ARHYEN CROUCHED IN THE MOONLIT DARKNESS BESIDE Ephraim and the masked man, observing their target location.

The masked man had led them to the outskirts of London, originally where those of the nobility and *old* money dwelled. Most of the mansions had been long since abandoned as the *nouveau riche* popularized the central area of town, near the market district the wealthy often frequented. Now all that was left were empty homes, some mere skeletal remains of their former glory, where vagrants lived until the Watch came through to chase them out. Ornate iron fences still loomed on either side of the streets, more sturdy than the homes they guarded.

The yard of the mansion standing before them strewn with old furniture and other refuse, cast aside as the abandoned homes were looted for any valuables that might have been left behind. The wood of the building, painted charcoal gray, had long since started to rot and warp, though the building still had sturdy-looking doors. While some of the windows retained their glass, it did not matter, because boards had been nailed up from the inside. Arhyen could see soft light peeking out from behind their slats, though as far as he'd been previously aware, the homes in the area no longer had electricity supplied to them.

A sudden noise caught Arhyen's ear. "What was that?" he whispered frantically. It had sounded like a woman's scream, muffled by the walls of the home.

"That was Liliana," the masked man stated emotionlessly. He'd yet to reveal his face, and Arhyen was finding him increasingly strange. His speech was often disjointed, and lacked the proper emphasis on certain words and syllables, yet when his speech was clear, he spoke with a high class mien that hinted at a thorough education.

Arhyen began to stand, ready to rush toward the house, but the masked man reached out and grabbed him by the arm. Arhyen pulled against him. If that scream was Liliana, he needed to go to her. There was no telling what harm might befall her while they waited out in the dark. When his arm did not come free, he pulled again, sending a jolt of pain across his body to his wounded shoulder. The masked man's grip was unbelievably strong. He could not tug free, no matter how hard he tried.

"I do not intend to let her come to any harm," the masked man explained calmly.

"She's coming to harm *now*," Arhyen argued, bordering on frenzy.

"Arhyen *think*," Ephraim cut in, still crouched in the same position. "We must be organized if we hope to rescue her. Rushing in without a plan is suicide. We cannot help her if we are dead."

Arhyen knew Ephraim was right, but couldn't seem to calm himself. Something terrible was happening to Liliana right that moment, and he couldn't just stand idly by. It was all his fault she was in there in the first place.

Releasing Arhyen's arm, the masked man explained, "I will enter through the front of the building to create a distraction. The two of you will wait ten minutes before entering through the back. Keep to the lower-level of the house as you search for Liliana. I do not believe the upper levels are in use, due to structural disintegration."

Arhyen was more than ready to go ahead with the plan, but Ephraim stood and crossed his arms. "And just how are we supposed to trust you? For all we know, *we* may be the actual distraction, so that you might kidnap Liliana for yourself."

The masked man stood eerily still. "If that were my intent, I would have taken her long ago."

"I believe him," Arhyen interrupted, hoping to quickly convince Ephraim. "He led us to Victor Ashdown, and I believe," he turned his gaze to the masked man, "he was the one to kill Clayton Blackwood's men, before leaving them on his front lawn."

The masked man answered with a slight nod, confirming Arhyen's suspicions. He'd already known that Viola was likely only claiming credit for the deaths, and that only left one suspect. A suspect who moved unnaturally fast, and seemed to be stronger than any man should be.

"Let's go," Arhyen demanded.

Ephraim didn't look happy about it, but he nodded. The masked man left them without another word, making his way toward the front door like a graceful shadow. Not wanting to waste any more time, Arhyen turned and led the way toward the back of the dilapidated mansion. He hadn't heard any more screams, but he found that fact even more troubling than if he had. At least screams meant Liliana was still alive.

Pushing his satchel into a more convenient position, he ran, weaving his way amongst the rubble, seeking out another way into the structure. His shoulder screamed at him from the extra movement, but it had at least stopped bleeding. If he survived the night, he'd make it a point to never get stabbed again. It really was quite vexing.

He slowed as a large covered porch came into view, dominating the backside of the building. Ephraim reached his side, and they both observed the porch for a moment. It was difficult to tell with the shadows cast by the porch's wooden roof, but there seemed to be only one door, and several boarded up windows. Entering either would likely take time, and the masked man had requested they join him in ten minutes. They needed to get moving.

Taking care to move silently now that they were within hearing range of the mansion, they both approached the porch stairs, then stepped cautiously onto the rotten wood, Arhyen leading the way.

Ephraim followed close behind him as he tiptoed toward the only visible door, bordered by the boarded up windows. The wood creaked and groaned perilously beneath his feet, threatening to give out. He heaved a sigh of relief as they reached the door. He tried the door-knob, knowing it couldn't be *that* simple. *Locked,* as expected. He was skilled at lock-picking, but didn't have the appropriate tools on him, nor did he currently have the patience.

Shouting erupted from within the building. Had the masked man made his move? Loud thuds and the sound of shattering glass joined in to create a distracting cacophony. With a nod of understanding to each other, he and Ephraim stepped back from the door, then charged as one, ramming it with their shoulders. The door burst open, its flimsy lock unable to hold up to the impact.

A man inside, holding a pistol, turned to them in surprise. Arhyen barely had time to blink as Ephraim flew through the doorway, straightening his hand to chop the man on the side of the neck, instantly rendering him unconscious.

Ephraim looked down at the man now sprawled on the stained carpeting. "Splitting up is a risk, but we'll stand a better chance of finding Liliana," he stated, as if trying to make up his mind on a previously internal debate.

"We split up," Arhyen replied.

Should they meet with force, splitting up might end badly, but it increased the chances of at least one of them being able to save her. He only had his single dagger, but could defend himself one on one if it came to it. Facing someone with a pistol was another story, but he couldn't waste time worrying about it.

They walked silently to the end of the narrow hallway that led in from the door, looked from side to side to see if any more men stood guard, then took off in opposite directions.

Sounds of fighting could still be heard near the front door, so Arhyen ignored that direction and hurried toward the back right side of the building. The wood paneled walls had all been stripped of their paintings, leaving slightly lighter rectangles on the wall in their place, and the carpet was torn up and moldy, but this portion of the house was otherwise unremarkable. He saw no signs of human life, likely because they'd all gone to meet the attack at the front door. He knew the masked man was strong and fast, but could he really take down an entire building full of armed assailants? There was always the possibility that only a few guards had been in place inside the mansion, but it seemed unlikely since the fight was still going on. He jumped as a pistol fired, thinking that perhaps the masked man had been hit, but the fighting continued.

He turned left down a hallway, then kept running. He neared another bend, then skidded to a halt as someone came into view. It wasn't a man like he'd expected, but a woman in a white coat carrying a folder of papers. At first he thought it might be Viola, then realized this woman was older, with gray streaks in her dark hair. Her eyes widened as she saw Arhyen.

Knowing he couldn't let her get away to bring the guards down upon him, he dove forward and tackled her. The papers in her arms went flying into the air to rain down on them as Arhyen wrestled her to the floor.

"Where is Liliana?" he growled down at her.

She struggled beneath him, to little avail. Giving up, she huffed, "The automaton?"

He nodded.

"Down the hall, take a right, then it's the door at the end," she grumbled. "Now please get off me. There's a man in a mask killing all of the guards and I want to get the hell out of here."

Well at least it didn't seem she'd report him. He lifted himself off her, then allowed her to run past, leaving her scattered papers behind.

Hoping he hadn't made a mistake in letting her live, he continued his search. He took the first right as instructed. At the end of the hall, there was a closed door with light shining through underneath it. He continued to run at full speed. Upon reaching it, he lifted his foot and kicked the door in as he reached it. The impact sent a thrill of pain up his leg to his spine, but he barely noticed it. The door slammed against the back wall, and he tumbled into a white room that looked like some sort of surgery. He forced himself to his feet, not taking the time to scan the entire room since he'd found what he was looking for. Strapped to a table a few paces ahead of him, was Liliana.

He ran forward, his heart racing. Her body was perfectly still. *Too* still.

Standing by her side, he began undoing her restraints, unable to bring himself to check her for signs of life. He couldn't even bring himself to look at her face. She wore a flimsy white nightgown, baring her thin arms to the bright light of the room. A trickle of blood marred the arm closest to him.

"Please be alive," he rasped, frantically releasing the last of the restraints.

"Arhyen?" a weak voice questioned.

His gaze whipped up to Liliana's face. Her eyes were open just a sliver, watching him.

He heaved a huge sigh of relief.

"Look-" she began, her voice barely above a whisper, then someone hit him in the back of his head with a heavy object. He fell to the ground, pain radiating through his skull, and everything went black.

CHAPTER 17

Arhyen knelt cradling his hands to his face, but couldn't seem to clear away his dizziness. Acting purely on instinct, he lowered his hands to brace himself against the concrete floor, then kicked out behind him. His boot grazed something, and there was a feminine grunt of pain. His vision finally cleared enough for him to glance over his shoulder, finding Viola standing above him, looking crazed with a thick glass apothecary bottle gripped in her right hand. She seemed to now be favoring her left leg as she recovered from the kick, but it hadn't been enough to upend her.

Snarling, she threw her arm back in preparation for another hit. Arhyen knew he wouldn't be able to move out of the way in time. Her arm sailed downward, then a white shape dove from the table and tackled her to the ground.

Finally Arhyen's faculties returned to him, and he was able to stumble to his feet. He staggered toward the two women, just as Liliana straddled Viola and ripped the bottle from her grasp. The bottle now in her clutches, Liliana brought it speeding toward Viola's face as the other woman cowered in fear. It would have possibly been a killing blow, but Liliana seemed to be dizzy, making her aim a little off. The bottle hit the floor beside Viola's face and shattered.

"Hey!" someone shouted from the doorway behind Arhyen.

He turned, still feeling somewhat unsteady on his feet, to see the scar-faced thug from the gambling establishment, the one who'd been present when Arhyen held Viola at knifepoint in the alley. In retrospect, he should have slit her throat that night, but it was too late to think about it now. Perhaps he'd still get a chance after he dealt with the new threat.

He turned to fully face his assailant, hoping Liliana was well enough to handle Viola. He desperately wanted to aid her, but would do her little good if the massive man standing in the doorway managed to get a hold of him. His head was still screaming, echoed dully by his wounded shoulder, yet he had no choice but to fight. He crouched into a defensive stance, prepared for the attack, but it never came. A long blade shot out the middle of the man's chest. He slumped to the floor as the blade withdrew, revealing the masked man standing calmly behind him.

Distracted by the scene in front of him, Arhyen hadn't heard anyone approach, but suddenly felt a presence at his back. He turned just in time to see a bruised and battered Viola hold up a shiny silver scalpel to stab him, then a delicate hand reared up behind her and jammed a broken bottle into the side of her neck.

Viola sputtered. Blood spewed from her mouth to mingle with her perfectly red lips. She coughed more blood, then fell to the ground with the broken bottle still protruding from her skin.

Her fall revealed Liliana, wide eyed with shock, her hand still in the air where it had gripped the bottle before stabbing it into Viola. She swayed on her feet. Arhyen reflexively stepped over Viola to gather Liliana quickly into his arms, though his wounded shoulder protested. She felt so small, and trembled from either fear or exhaustion. Probably both.

"Well it seems I missed all the fun," a voice said from the doorway.

Liliana still in his arms, Arhyen turned to see Ephraim now standing next to the masked man, appearing unharmed.

Ephraim glanced at the masked man warily. "I saw the state of the entry way," he commented. "How did you manage to defeat them all?"

"He's an automaton," a small voice said beside Arhyen's ear.

He pulled away from Liliana just enough to see her face, still supporting her to keep her from falling. The flimsy nightgown barely covered her, but he had no coat to offer.

Not seeming to notice her state of undress, Liliana continued, "I realized when we saw him run from Clayton and Viola. He was too fast to be human. He escaped because he was able to jump to the top of the wall like I was."

Arhyen turned to the masked man for confirmation.

He touched a finger to the top of his mask where it met his dark hairline, as if tipping his hat, which he'd lost at some point in the fighting, then bowed. "The lady is correct. I am an artificial life, created by the alchemists of the *London Network*."

At the notorious name, everyone gasped.

"I am referred to as *Codename Hamlet*," he continued, stepping over the corpse of the scarred man to come further into the room, "after the failed project that would have resulted in more of my kind, but you may simply call me Hamlet. Though I am an automaton, I am not quite like our young lady here. I was created to be a soldier, or, more accurately, a weapon."

"So Viola's claim that she was a part of the *LN* was a lie?" Arhyen questioned. Things slowly began to add up in his mind, but there were still so many unanswered questions.

"Not quite," Hamlet answered. He moved to stand over Viola's body as it bled onto the floor. Looking down at the woman's corpse, he continued, "Many of London's business leaders are involved in the *Network*, though they mostly hold lesser roles, and do not have access to all information. Viola was no different. Unhappy with her lack of power, she hired many spies within the Network, and gained numerous supporters among the lesser members. When it was revealed that the *London Network* planned to interfere with the work of Fairfax Breckenridge, she disagreed with our proposed tactics. Her faction branched off on its own, to meet its own ends. Clayton Blackwood was among that group."

"Then who killed my father?" Liliana questioned weakly. "Was it Viola's faction, or was it *you*?"

"I do not know who killed your father," Hamlet admitted. "Our plan had only just begun when news of his disappearance began to spread. Our intent had been to obtain his research before it reached the public, by any means necessary."

Ephraim snorted. "So basically you intended to kill him, but someone else got to it first."

Hamlet nodded. "That is correct, though I was not involved in that side of the mission. My orders were to observe Viola and her followers. They had abducted Victor Ashdown, who was involved in Breckenridge's work. We hoped to find him to ensure that he had not hidden any information on Breckenridge's research."

Arhyen shook his head in disbelief. Liliana was perfectly still, steadied in his arms, quietly taking in the news. "If you already knew that Ashdown had been abducted," he began, "then why did you prompt us with that note to search for him?"

Hamlet nodded, acknowledging that Arhyen had correctly interpreted his intent. "It was learned that Clayton Blackwood had tortured and killed Victor Ashdown for information on Breckenridge's research. I also knew that Ashdown had been involved in some capacity in developing said research. Therefore, I needed to learn what Blackwood knew, and who else he might have told. Unfortunately, after murdering Victor Ashdown, Blackwood had not acted, aside from hiring someone to steal research." He nodded in Arhyen's direction, acknowledging that he knew Arhyen was that *someone*. "You were the catalyst I needed to spur him into action. You had brought Liliana to London, and I needed to see if Blackwood would attempt to obtain her. Sending both of you after Victor Ashdown guaranteed you would remain in Blackwood's sights. He would soon figure out just who Liliana was. If he tried to obtain her, I would know that Ashdown's side of the equation had not been released. If Blackwood knew of Ashdown's research, and was able to obtain Breckenridge's journal, he would not need Liliana. The fact that she was abducted has let me know that all is not lost. This splinter faction of the Network has not figured out how to complete Breckenridge's formulae."

"But they're all dead," Arhyen argued. "What does it matter now what they knew?"

Hamlet nodded in acceptance of the rational viewpoint. "It would not matter, if those in this building were the only parties involved, but Viola was just one of many. Some are not even known to the *LN* itself. It is imperative that this information does not reach certain hands."

Ephraim cleared his throat. "If you wanted them out on the streets in Blackwood's sight, then why plant the note in the dead man's pocket? Incriminating Arhyen for murder seems counterproductive."

Hamlet turned his head toward Ephraim. "To pique your interest, of course. I had already observed your arrangement with Arhyen, and wanted to ensure you'd be involved. You have access to resources out of his reach."

Ephraim sighed. "So we played right into your hands on every front?"

Hamlet simply nodded, not bothering to elaborate further.

Arhyen felt dizzy and tired, and all he wanted in that moment was to get Liliana out of that room, but there was still a question he needed to ask. "What is all of this for? Why is Breckenridge's research worth dying over?"

"He created synthetic emotions," Liliana answered for him. "That's what my father made, what he called my *soul*. He used a compound created by Ashdown, the *Advector Serum*, to administer them. Nothing I feel is truly real." Her voice was perfectly even as she spoke, showing no emotion whatsoever. It was her tone that scared Arhyen the most.

Hamlet nodded again. "Such compounds could be used in a myriad of ways, though the end result would always be the same. *Chaos*. The Network could not allow these things to come to pass."

Liliana stepped away from Arhyen, though she still seemed unsteady on her feet. "Viola took my blood," she explained. "She claimed that it could be refined to produce those same compounds. It should probably be destroyed."

She stared directly at Hamlet. "And you should probably kill me."

Arhyen turned to her in shock. "Liliana, you can't-" he began, but Hamlet cut him off.

"That was a ruse," he explained, his gaze on Liliana. "One I apologize for. It was part of the initiative I took to force Blackwood into acting. He *happened* upon information that should he fail to acquire the formulae, your blood would suffice, though it would be a limited supply, obviously. I apologize for endangering you, but it seemed the most simple option."

"Simple option, my arse," Ephraim muttered to himself.

Arhyen shared his sentiments. He looked back to Liliana, who appeared pale and utterly dejected. Why would she give in to death so easily?

"Be that as it may," Hamlet continued, still addressing Liliana. "Your brain is still dangerous, but at the same time, may prove incredibly useful. You will be offered a position as an alchemist for the *London Network*."

Arhyen frowned. "Let me guess, if she refuses, you'll kill her?"

Hamlet nodded. "The same offer stands for both of you," he glanced at Ephraim, then back to Arhyen. "It is a risk leaving you alive, but many feel you would prove more useful to the Network in life, than in death."

Ephraim scoffed. "And who are these people that feel we would prove useful? I already have an occupation, you know."

Seeming unfazed by Ephraim's attitude, Hamlet explained. "You will both continue your lives as you have, and remain in your . . . " He glanced at Arhyen. " . . . *occupations*. The *Network* will be in contact. You will obey all orders, and maintain utter confidentiality."

"Or we'll be killed," Arhyen added. He had no doubt

that Hamlet would kill them right there if they refused. Judging by Ephraim's earlier comments, he'd already killed an entire room of men, and seemed no worse for wear. "What about Liliana?" he pressed.

Hamlet tilted his head to the side. "She has been offered a prestigious position with the *Network*, but if she chooses, she may remain in your care . . . though she will be called on from time to time, not only for information, but so that we might study just what Fairfax Breckenridge created."

"You won't *study* her," Arhyen stated defensively, moving to stand in front of Liliana. "She's a person, not an experiment."

"It's fine," Liliana muttered from behind him. She stepped forward. "I *am* an experiment. I was grown in a laboratory. My emotions are synthetic. I have no soul."

Her attitude suddenly making sense to him, Arhyen frowned. He was an idiot for not realizing it before. She'd just received confirmation that her father really hadn't given her a soul. He'd given her emotions so that she might feel like any other human, but they were emotions created by alchemy.

"There is one thing that I still don't understand," Ephraim interjected, stroking his chin in thought. How he was managing to stay so calm was completely beyond Arhyen's comprehension. "Why did you steal those items? I'm assuming the stolen *gemstone* was actually created by Victor Ashdown. The alchemical tomes also make sense in regards of eliminating information, but what of the burial urn and the antique dagger?"

"The urn contained the ashes of one of the greatest minds of this century," Hamlet replied, "though I am not at liberty to say any more than that. The gemstones generate electricity, as I'm sure you've gathered. Their power can be used to fuel various experiments, just as they have fueled this makeshift laboratory," he gestured at the room with a gloved hand. "The dagger, I thought was pretty, and exceedingly well made."

Ephraim balked. "You stole it because it was *pretty?*"

Hamlet reached into his coat, then produced an ornate dagger. The hilt was gold and jewel encrusted. He withdrew it from the gold sheath to reveal a thin, silver blade. After observing the dagger for a moment, he resheathed it and returned it to his coat.

"The three of you must leave now," Hamlet stated. "I must destroy all evidence of what took place this night before any of the authorities happen upon us." He turned to Ephraim. "Should any of this come to light, you will be expected to cover it up."

Ephraim glared at him. "That's a contradiction of the oath I took to the Queen. My loyalty is to the Watch."

"Your loyalty is to yourself," Hamlet countered, "and to the *Network.* Your two priorities are to stay alive, and to protect classified information. Now please leave. I'll be in touch."

Ephraim turned and stormed out of the doorway, hopping effortlessly over the dead man still lying there, without another word.

Arhyen turned to Liliana, who stared down at her feet. "Liliana," he began, but she didn't look up. "*Liliana,*" he said more forcefully.

She seemed to snap back into reality at that.

He wanted to just pick her up and carry her out of the room right that moment, but Hamlet had given her a choice. It wasn't right for him to make it for her. She could either work as an alchemist for the *London Network,* or she could stay with him.

"What do you want to do?" he asked, doing his best to be patient.

She glanced back at Viola's corpse, then to the dead man near the doorway, then to Hamlet. "I want to go with you," she stated evenly.

Arhyen's heart nearly stopped. She was staring at Hamlet when she said it. Did she really want to go be an alchemist for the *LN*? He supposed he couldn't really blame her, it wasn't like the life he could offer her was overly grand.

"If that's what you choose . . . " he trailed off, trying to keep the sadness out of his voice and failing.

Liliana startled, then turned toward him. "No," she corrected. "I mean I want to go with *you*, if you'll still have me now that we know . . . " she ended, her voice snagging on what was left unsaid. *Now that we know I don't have a soul.*

He grabbed her and pulled her close, sliding his good arm back around her waist. "It doesn't change a thing," he assured. He looked back to Hamlet, then breathed a sigh of relief as Hamlet stepped aside and gestured for them to leave.

Arhyen started forward, taking Liliana with him, but she paused as they reached the other automaton. Hamlet's eyes met hers through the mask, and something seemed to pass between them. Something that Arhyen would never truly comprehend.

"There's one thing I still don't understand," she said softly, her eyes still on Hamlet.

He nodded for her to continue.

"Viola claimed that my father created sadness, happiness, rage, and," she hesitated, "love. Yet, those are not the only emotions I feel. I became quite acquainted with fear while I was strapped to that table." She glanced back at the table in question.

Though they could not see Hamlet's face, Arhyen sensed the automaton was smiling. "You and I may be artificial creations," he replied, "but that does not mean we are incapable of learning and adapting. Whether we simply mimic humanity, or have developed instincts of our own, will forever remain unclear. As you acquire further experiences, it is likely you will continue to change and adapt."

She seemed about ready to leave, then shook her head. "I have one more question, actually."

Hamlet nodded again for her to go on, even though he had evidence disposal to see to.

"It's been years since the formulae were administered to me with the *Advector Serum*," she explained, "yet my emotions have not faded. They come and go as I react to external stimuli."

Arhyen flinched as Hamlet lifted a gloved hand, but he simply tapped it gently on the top of Liliana's head. "Your brain is very similar to a true human brain. It only needed to experience the chemical reactions of emotions once for them to become habitual behaviors. The emotions you feel now are a result of your mind's abilities to learn instincts."

She nodded somberly, as if that was the answer she'd expected, then turned her gaze to Arhyen. Interpreting her wordless request, he guided her toward the door. They walked toward the scarred man's dead body, then he swept her off her feet, cradling her in his arms so she wouldn't have to struggle over the gargantuan corpse with her shorter legs.

"I'll be in touch," Hamlet stated as they left the room, and Hamlet, behind.

"Of course you will," Arhyen muttered bitterly.

He continued to carry Liliana, and she did not protest, as they made their way toward the back entrance unmolested. Once outside, they found Ephraim waiting for them.

Arhyen continued to walk across the rubble strewn lawn of the mansion toward the street. Ephraim fell into step at his side.

Once they'd put some distance between themselves and the mansion, Arhyen's gaze flicked to Ephraim. "What are we going to do about all of this?" he asked quietly. Liliana remained silent in his arms, though he could sense her eyes peering up at him.

Ephraim glanced over and met his gaze. "What do you think?" The ire Ephraim felt about being ordered to betray his oaths was clear in his pale eyes.

The question didn't need an answer. There was a certain knowing in both men's expressions. They were going to join the *London Network*, then they were going to take the organization down from the inside.

As they continued to walk, the building behind them went up in flames, erasing all evidence of the strangest night in Arhyen's life.

CHAPTER 18

The next morning the sun rose, just like it did every day, but the light seemed somehow different to Arhyen. The city he'd always called home seemed somehow different too. It was hard to relax when you knew a secret network was out there, running things behind the scenes while creating unstoppable killing machines like Hamlet. Not only that, but they had the knowledge to create synthetic emotions. Though they'd wanted to keep said knowledge out of Viola's hands, there was no saying how the *LN* might employ such power. They'd already condoned a slew of killings, so Arhyen could not trust that whatever they had planned was good.

He leaned against the couch where he'd slept, sipping a cooling cup of black tea. He still couldn't quite believe he was alive and back in his apartment, after all that had happened. He'd cleaned up his shoulder wound, and other than that, he didn't even have any major injuries. He still expected a questioning from the Watch in regards to Clayton's claims, but as Mr. Blackwood was now *missing* himself, there was little evidence against Arhyen. He glanced at the bed where Liliana still slept. There was little evidence of *anything*, since Hamlet had burned it all. He briefly wondered if Clayton's body would still be in the smelter building, but dismissed the idea. Clayton's death would have been covered up like all the rest.

His gaze remained on Liliana. They'd arrived home in the wee hours of the morning and he'd put her to bed. She hadn't spoken a single word since they'd left Hamlet and the mansion of horrors behind. She'd lost a lot of blood, and was understandably weakened, but he did not think that was the reason she refrained from speaking, nor was it the reason she was still in bed now.

He looked down at the journal in his lap. It was the one Liliana had written, filled with the formulae that so many had recently died for. The *LN* didn't know that he had it, as far as he knew, but he'd have to keep it well hidden if he hoped to keep his secret. It wasn't that he wanted to keep the formulae away from them, they already had the *real* journal, after all, but it was always best to have just as much information as your enemies. If not more.

He rose from the sofa and walked into the nearby bathroom, stopping along the way to reach into his satchel. Sealing himself in the small room, he set his teacup on the edge of the sink. He then crouched with the journal under one arm, pulling a slender lock picking tool out of the front pocket of his charcoal waistcoat. He ran the fingers of his free hand around the edges of a single tile in the middle of the floor, then inserted the tool under one corner, lifting the edge of the tile enough to get a hold on it. He lifted the tile and set it aside, then retrieved the tiny key he always kept on his person from the same pocket that had held the lockpick. He used the key to unlock the small safe that resided in a cavern carved into the apartment's foundation. He opened the lid of the safe and inserted the journal next to the original note from Liliana's father, and a few small purses of coin. Next he removed Victor Ashdown's electricity stone, previously retrieved from his satchel, from his pants pocket and placed it beside the journal. The stone gave him hope that Hamlet had not rifled through his satchel, since it had remained within upon the satchel's return. Either that, or Hamlet was testing him in some way, waiting to see what he would do with the stone and the journal. He would keep them both hidden regardless.

Chirani Ashdown had claimed that she had several more of the stones hidden away, but Arhyen thought it likely she would not have those stones for long, since Hamlet had gone to the trouble of stealing others. He only hoped Hamlet would not harm the girl in the process.

He sat back and leaned against the wall of the bathtub, thinking about Hamlet. He was an automaton, like Liliana, yet he was *nothing* like her. Still, he couldn't help but wonder if Hamlet had been given emotions too. He didn't act like a normal automaton. He seemed to think for himself, and had a sense of humor, albeit a horrible one. He had even coveted a *pretty* dagger. Arhyen recalled the answers Hamlet had given Liliana, about how she could learn and evolve just like anyone else. He knew it to be true. He'd seen her evolve over the course of their adventure, as if she were acquiring new emotions right before his very eyes. He'd enjoyed seeing most of them on her, save the sadness and despair.

Arhyen shook away his thoughts. He locked the safe and returned the tile, then stood and retrieved his tea, which had grown cold. He went back into the living room and sat back on the sofa, prepared to wait as long as Liliana needed.

Liliana turned over in bed, then finally opened her eyes to stare up at the ceiling. She'd been fully aware when the sun rose, then crept across the sky to eventually fall once more. Arhyen had made some noise at a few different points, and she vaguely recalled Ephraim visiting, but mostly things were silent. She didn't want to get up. There was no reason. She'd suspected all along that she might not really have a soul, but hearing such a thing for certain was another matter entirely. Even if she had managed to further develop her emotions on her own, how could she live without a soul? How could she *feel* without one? Did she even deserve to do either? Her eyes closed in despair.

After a few moments, she turned her head to the side and opened her eyes a sliver, then jumped. Arhyen was standing right beside the bed, fully dressed in black trousers, and a black, high collared shirt, topped by a charcoal waistcoat and short black jacket. On his head rested his bowler cap. Was he leaving? She stared at him blankly.

"It's about time," he commented, straightening the black ascot at his neck.

"Time for what?" she mumbled.

"Time for you to get out of bed and start your lessons."

She opened her eyes fully to stare at him. "Lessons?"

He raised his eyebrows toward the brim of his hat like she was being incredibly daft. "Don't tell me you've given up on your dream of thieving already."

She turned onto her stomach and buried her face in the pillow. "That was more me just wanting to be useful," she replied, the fabric muffling her voice. "I don't really want to be a thief. I don't really want to be *anything*."

In one smooth movement, he whipped the covers off her. She curled into a ball, pressing the pillow over her face with both hands. He sighed loudly, then wrestled the pillow from her grip. She sat up with a huff and glared at him, blowing her wayward hair out of her face.

He crossed his arms and stared down at her. "We had a *deal*, and I'm not about to let you rob me of my half of the bargain. I need an apprentice now more than ever if we're to face what is to come." He sat down on the bed beside her.

She turned toward him, unable to help her curiosity. "What's to come?" she questioned.

"Rule number one of being a thief," he stated, holding a finger in the air. "Never admit defeat. If there's a fight to be had, you must always fight it."

"I thought rule number one was to only steal from the wealthy," she countered.

He rolled his eyes. "Rule number four then."

She crossed her legs beneath her, then realized she was still wearing the flimsy night dress Viola had put her in. She tugged the fabric down to cover her knees, feeling suddenly exposed.

Not seeming to notice, Arhyen continued, "Now are you going to take away my number three, or what?"

She narrowed her eyes at him. "Number three?"

"Having a trusted partner," he reminded her. "I *thought* I'd found one, but it seems she might make me do all of the work myself."

She bristled at that. "I'm still trustworthy!" she argued.

"Good." He removed his cap to reveal his shaggy brown hair, then placed it on her head. "We have a meeting to attend within the hour, so you better get dressed."

"Meeting?" she questioned, lightly touching the hat on her head.

He winked at her, then stood. "All shall reveal itself in time. Get dressed and I'll make you a sandwich."

She looked down at her lap for a few seconds, then

made up her mind. She might not have much to live for, but if Arhyen needed her help, the least she could do was give it to him. She stood, then glanced around the apartment for her dress. She groaned when she realized it had likely met its demise in Hamlet's fire.

Noting her distress from his post in the kitchen, Arhyen turned and pointed the knife he was using to slice bread at the couch. "I believe you'll find *those* well suited to tonight's activities."

She looked where the knife pointed to find a pile of neatly folded black clothing on one of the sofa cushions. She walked toward it curiously. There didn't seem to be enough fabric to compose a proper dress like her lost one.

Knife still in hand, Arhyen made a shooing gesture. "Go on now, we haven't got all night."

She nodded, quickly snatched the clothing, then hurried into the bathroom to change.

After gently shutting the door behind her, she took a moment to peer into the small, circular mirror. She was a mess. There were bloodstains on her nightgown and skin, and grime beneath her fingernails. Her hair was snarled and dull with dirt. She glanced at the bathtub, wondering if she had time to clean herself. She took a final glance in the mirror, then decided there was no choice. She'd just need to be quick.

She set down her pile of clothing on the sink, then hurried over to the tub, quickly removing Arhyen's hat and her dirty shift. Glancing back at the door to ensure she'd locked it, she plugged the drain, turned on the water full blast, and quickly hopped in, not checking to see if it was a bearable temperature. The icy water nearly took her breath away, but soon became bearable as more hot was added to the cold. Once the water reached an acceptable tempera-ture, she shut it off. Procuring a yellow bar of soap from the rim of the tub, she began to scrub herself, imagining that she was scrubbing away the memories of the past day and evening. Not *all* of the memories though. She didn't mind the memory of Arhyen rescuing her, and of his expression when he'd realized she was still alive. *Those* memories she would keep, even if they only meant something to her.

She washed her hair quickly, beginning to feel oddly giddy. Though she was overwhelmed with the revelations Viola had provided, she couldn't help but be a little excited about the night ahead. Perhaps that excitement was artificially constructed, but she *felt* it all the same.

Thoroughly cleansed, she unplugged the drain and stood, then tugged a towel off a nearby hook on the wall. She frowned at it, then the empty space of wall where no more towels hung. The single towel had to be Arhyen's . . . but there was nothing else to dry herself with. Figuring she'd apologize for the intrusion later, she dried herself off, then wrapped the towel around her hair. She stepped out of the tub onto the bare tile floor, then reached for the new clothing.

The first article was a black shirt with buttons running up the front. She observed it for a moment, then moved onto the next pieces of clothing, fresh undergarments, finding that receiving them did not make her blush as much the second time around. Although, she really would have to find a way to do her own shopping in the future. She couldn't expect Arhyen to buy her undergarments forever.

She frowned when she realized there were no stockings, then reached for the last article of clothing, unfolding the fabric to find a pair of black trousers. They appeared to be just her size, and clearly designed for a woman, though she wasn't aware women could wear such things.

Feeling oddly exhilarated, she donned the clothing, then cleared the steam from the mirror to look at herself.

Though the mirror was only able to provide a view of the shirt, and not the trousers, everything seemed to fit. Wanting to ask Arhyen a million questions, she combed her fingers through her wet hair, grabbed his hat, and returned to the living area in a waft of steam.

Arhyen looked up from the sofa and grinned as he saw her. "I wasn't sure the clothes would fit properly," he admitted. "They're made for women of the equestrian crowd, as it's difficult to ride horses in skirts."

Liliana hopped from one bare foot to another, demonstrating the new clothes, then blushed in embarrassment. "It's odd being able to move so freely," she muttered.

Arhyen nodded, then gestured toward the sandwich he'd made her on the table. "That's the point. I'd like us to travel undetected tonight, and I didn't want you hindered by a dress." He glanced down at her bare feet. "There are boots to go with it too," he added.

She stood awkwardly for a moment, then hurried around the low table to take a seat on the sofa. Realizing she was being rude, she muttered, "Thank you for the clothing."

He lifted the sandwich plate from the table and handed it to her. "You can thank Ephraim. He's the one that picked everything out."

Her eyes widened and she nearly dropped her plate. "Why would Ephraim pick out my clothing?" she blurted.

Arhyen rolled his eyes. "Well I wasn't about to leave you unprotected while you slept, not after everything that happened. And Ephraim didn't fancy waiting around the apartment while *I* shopped."

Liliana's face felt like it was on fire. She was wearing undergarments picked out by *Ephraim*. It was embarrassing enough when Arhyen did it, but Ephraim? She wasn't sure she'd even be able to meet his eyes next time she saw him.

"There's no need to protect me," she managed to say after recovering from her initial shock. "I mean, I appreciate it, but you shouldn't have troubled yourself."

"That's what partners are for." He smiled, though there was a certain tension around his eyes that had never been there before.

Liliana sensed something amiss. Did he feel odd around her now that they knew the truth of what she was? She tried to formulate some way of asking him, but everything she could come up with seemed incredibly awkward. She looked down at the sandwich on her plate, having no desire to eat.

Finally, she settled on bluntness. Unable to lift her eyes to meet his, she asked, "Are you sure you're alright with me staying here? I will understand fully if you want me to leave. It will be no trouble for me to find another place to stay." So she'd settled for bluntness, *and* a minor lie. She just didn't want him to feel pressured into keeping her.

He took her sandwich plate suddenly and placed it on the table, then grabbed her hand. "Liliana," he began patiently, "what do you think a soul is?"

The question caught her off guard. She glanced up to see if he was joking, but his eyes were very serious, the tension around them remaining. "As far as I've been able to discern from my readings," she began, grasping for the correct words, "a soul is an intangible, immortal thing. It is responsible for morality, personality, and to a lesser extent, emotion, though most of emotion can be explained away as a result of lingering survival instincts."

"Now tell me," he replied, still grasping her hand in his. "Do you possess a sense of morality?"

She hesitated, but nodded. She was quite sure she knew right from wrong, and felt compelled to do *right*.

"Do you possess emotion?" he continued.

"Well yes, but—" she began to argue, but he cut her off.

"So you have morals and emotions," he stated, "and I can attest to the fact that you have a personality. Who is to say that you do not, therefore, possess a soul?"

"Because my emotions are artificial," she argued, though with no real passion behind it. She *wanted* to agree with him, but couldn't. "Everything about me is artificial, not a result of my immortal soul."

Arhyen gave her hand a squeeze. "Perhaps, but this all begs the question, do our inner tendencies compose our souls, or do our souls compose our inner tendencies?"

She frowned. "That doesn't make sense."

"No, but neither do souls." He winked at her. "There's really no saying if *any* of us have them. Souls may be an artificial construct as much as anything else. The argument is futile. You are here, you are alive, and you *care*. What does anything else matter?"

She opened her mouth to argue, and realized she could not.

"See?" he said. "Now why should I care whether or not my apprentice has a soul, when no one knows what a soul is, or even if they truly exist. It's silly to waste time over such trivialities. You have everything that's *important*, without argument."

She took a moment to think about what he'd said. Her hand was growing warm in his grasp, but she did not find it entirely unpleasant. She recalled her earlier excitement while she was getting dressed, and the despair she'd felt when she'd thought Arhyen had perished, coupled with her joy at seeing him alive. She also felt a very new emotion, one she felt a need to express.

"Arhyen," she began softly, thinking of how best to phrase her words.

He squeezed her hand again, seeming suddenly nervous. "Yes?" he asked, after a few seconds of silence.

She smiled softly. "When we were speaking the other night, you told me to let you know when I felt I could trust you," she explained. "I wasn't quite sure what you meant, or how I would *know* when such an occurrence took place, but I understand now."

He lifted his eyebrows in surprise. "You do?"

She nodded. "Yes, I believe the feeling in my chest right now is trust."

He grinned and shook his head. He opened his mouth as if to say something, then closed it.

She smiled, glad she was able to so succinctly express her feelings. She was also glad to see the tension had left Arhyen's face. He seemed suddenly relaxed, though oddly, he still held her hand.

"So what is our next mission?" she asked.

He waggled his eyebrows at her. "I told you, all will be revealed in time. Now eat your sandwich, we're going to be late." He let go of her hand and retrieved the plate for her.

She debated reminding him that she didn't *need* to eat, and if they were going to be late they could just leave right then, but she liked the way he was smiling at her. He leaned back against the sofa cushions, seeming at ease. She liked sitting with him, especially with a companionable mood in the air. So, despite the late hour, she took her time eating her sandwich. She was quite sure it was the best one yet.

CHAPTER 19

They hurried along down the dark streets. Arhyen was pleased to find that Liliana's new black boots were far more quiet than her previous ones. He was also pleased with how quickly she could move in the new outfit. She easily paced him as they hurried through the shadows, and likely would have left him in the dust if she knew where they were going. It was good he hadn't told her.

He was not sure if the *London Network* had a way of listening in on conversations in his apartment, but he hadn't been willing to risk giving anything away, just in case. They would need to come up with some sort of code from that point forward. He'd had more than the task of shopping to relay to Ephraim when he'd visited that morning, but he'd made a point of being quite vague with the requests. Ephraim had understood though, and if all went according to plan, would be waiting for them at the meeting place.

Arhyen would not risk heading straight there though, first he would need to be sure they weren't followed. He'd already noticed a highly suspect street urchin hanging around his door earlier that day. There was no good reason for the boy, a scruffy youth of around thirteen, to be there. Those of his ilk tended to stick to the market district during the day, either begging for coin, or covertly proffering it from wealthy pockets, but this child had remained outside for several hours, only to later be replaced by an older vagrant pretending to be asleep. Arhyen wouldn't be overly surprised if he was told that *every* vagrant in the city was in the employ of the *LN*.

Since they'd left the apartment, he'd noted echoing footsteps behind them numerous times. If Hamlet was the one following them, he doubted they could evade him, but he thought it unlikely that the automaton would be employed on such a menial task as keeping an eye on the *LN*'s newest forced recruits, nor would he be clumsy enough to alert them of his presence. No, they were likely being followed by other humans, just like those who loitered outside his apartment.

He veered across the dark street, making his way toward a fire escape on the side of a tall building. He silently guided Liliana to start climbing, then followed up after her, the cold metal of the rungs stinging his bare hands. As he ascended he thought he heard footsteps on the cobblestones below, but it was difficult to tell with the noise of their climb. Liliana had scurried ahead, and now waited atop the building for him. Reaching the end of the ladder, he peered at the street below. No one climbed the fire escape after them.

He boosted himself the rest of the way on top of the building, then moved away from the edge. "I hope you're not afraid of heights," he whispered as Liliana hurried to stay at his side.

She didn't appear afraid. She did, however, appear

monumentally confused. With her hair curled up in a bun and a black cap on her head, she'd be difficult to spot in a crowd, and just as difficult to spot atop a roof in the darkness, which was exactly what they were going for.

Not wanting to give their pursuers time to formulate a new plan, he grabbed Liliana's hand and traipsed across the solid roof of the building to the hatch access meant for maintenance workers. Dropping Liliana's hand, he made quick work of the lock with tools removed from his coat. He quietly opened the door, and down they went into the building, shutting the hatch gently behind them.

"Where are we going?" she whispered, glancing around the building's top story, a storage space for barrels of grain and hops.

"Down," he whispered, reclaiming her hand. No one ought to be in the brewery at this hour, though that wasn't the only reason he'd chosen that particular building to climb. He knew the cellar, where giant casks of ale were stored, had access to London's water drainage system. They could pass undetected through the network, arriving at their destination with the *LN* none the wiser.

They hurried out of the storage area and down wooden stairs to the main brewing room. Liliana glanced around in the darkness curiously. There was a sudden *thunk* upstairs. Had someone actually followed them onto the roof and into the building? Arhyen shook his head in irritation, then tugged Liliana forward toward the cellar entrance.

The hatch guarding the stairs was composed of massive double doors mounted into the brick floor, covering a space large enough to carry barrels in or out. Luckily there was no lock on the doors, and they only needed to open one side to slip through.

Arhyen crouched to lift the heavy wood, then held it open for Liliana. Once she disappeared into the darkness below, he hurried down the steps after her, shutting the hatch above his head, leaving them in total darkness. Knowing that searching for a light would likely alert whoever followed to their location, Arhyen fumbled about for Liliana's hand, accidentally brushing her leg, then her hip in the process. Once her hand was firmly in his, he started forward, keeping his free hand in front of him to avoid running into any of the barrels. The grate leading downward should be only a few steps ahead.

There, Arhyen stepped onto the grate, making the metal groan softly.

Footsteps sounded above them, more than one set. For the first time Arhyen wondered if perhaps it wasn't the *LN* following them. Perhaps some associates of Clayton's or Viola's were left over to enact vengeance.

He shook his head and stepped off the grate. There was nothing he could do about it now. If they could escape quickly, perhaps their pursuers would think they'd gone out the front door. He crouched, bringing Liliana down beside him, then let go of her hand to quietly move the grate, just enough to make space for them both to slip through. Footsteps sounded near the cellar doors, then murmured voices. The cellar door creaked open.

Nervous sweat beading on his brow, he helped Liliana down onto the steel ladder beneath the grate. Fortunately not asking questions, she quickly ascended. Arhyen followed her, slowly sliding the grate back into place as the light of a lantern filled the cellar.

He was scarcely breathing as he waited at the top of the ladder. The grate would mostly conceal his presence, but if the lantern bearer lowered the light to peer through, he would be caught. He could hurry downward, but his progress would make at least a small amount of noise, and it might alert whoever pursued them.

Footsteps neared, bringing the light of the lantern with them. Arhyen silently prayed that Liliana would not call up to him, wondering why he hadn't joined her at the bottom.

The lantern holder stepped right on top of the grate, then kept walking. Arhyen heaved a sigh of relief, then nearly cursed out loud as a second person moved toward the grate and lowered a light.

Noises be damned, he half stepped, half slid the rest of the way down the ladder. By touch alone, he found Liliana waiting at the bottom, just as the grate above was lifted and tossed aside with a loud clatter. Taking her hand in his, he used his right hand to feel along the wall of the underground canal. The water rushed along peacefully to their left. He knew the walkways on either side of the water were only roughly three steps wide, so he kept close to the wall, guiding Liliana to do the same. He'd traveled the route many times before. If they could reach the complex maze of waterways roughly twenty steps ahead, they might be able to lose their pursuers in the dark. He had a small lantern in his satchel, but didn't dare use it.

The sound of feet hitting the concrete at the base of the ladder made him flinch. Just a few more seconds until the first turn.

The wall disappeared beneath his hand, signaling the bend in the drainage canal. He turned it, walked a few steps, then kicked his left foot to the side, searching for the narrow walkway that crossed the water. He found it just as the light neared the corridor they'd turned down.

Quickly scampering across with gritted teeth, he waited for the moment he'd step too far to one side and fall off the walkway, but it never came. Liliana seemed to have no trouble following in the darkness right behind him. As soon as he stepped onto the next platform, he regained Liliana's hand and ran full-speed forward, knowing there was a corridor directly ahead of him.

They continued on like that, taking numerous turns, as the lantern light fell further and further behind them. Eventually they lost their pursuers in the maze of canals. He hoped whoever followed them stayed lost down there forever. He waited another minute to be sure they were alone, then took a deep breath and plastered his back against the nearest wall. The lack of light was starting to get to him. Figuring it was now worth the slight risk, he fumbled through his satchel for his lantern and matchbox. He set the lantern on the ground and kneeled, then struck a match.

Liliana's face illuminated across from him in the flare of light. She'd kneeled on the other side of the lantern.

"Don't tell me you can actually see in the dark," he whispered, lowering the match to the wick.

She shook her head, obviously not comprehending his sarcasm. "No, I suppose I just have good spacial awareness and hearing."

He stood with the lantern and raised an eyebrow at her. "So you truly had no trouble following my lead?"

She rose and shook her head again. "No," she smirked, "you're quite loud."

He balked. Had she actually just made a joke? He suddenly felt as if the entire foray through the drainage canals was worth it. He held the lantern aloft and looked around. If he'd navigated correctly, the grate nearest the meeting place was only a short distance away.

He began walking again while Liliana followed silently behind him. When she'd first asked him to teach her his thieving ways, he had not thought it possible. An apprentice would simply slow him down, or get him caught. She'd proven him wrong on both counts. Once she learned the ropes, she'd be a far superior thief, just given her physical assets.

"Can you tell me where we're going now?" she whispered from behind him.

He barely heard her voice over the gentle flow of water beside them. He took another turn into a dry corridor that would lead to the proper grate. Or what should be the proper grate. He'd traveled the drainage canals countless times, but never whilst running away from someone, with no light to guide him.

"We're going to a meeting," he explained softly, feeling nervous even though there was no way someone from the *LN* could be present to listen to them.

"Does this have something to do with what you and Ephraim are planning?" she asked.

He stopped so abruptly that Liliana ran into his back, nearly jostling the lantern from his grip. He turned so the light would illuminate her face. She appeared utterly serious.

"How on earth did you figure that out?" he asked. He'd barely even communicated with Ephraim, not wanting the *LN* to catch on.

She tilted her cap covered head. "Last night when we left the burning building behind," she explained, "I saw the look you two gave each other. It was a mixture of determination and ire. There is no way such a look could have held no hidden meaning."

He smiled at her, then turned to continue walking. "You know, perhaps instead of becoming a thief, you should ask Ephraim to train you as a detective."

"No, thank you," she answered softly. "I don't care for the uniforms."

He bit his lip to hold in an abrupt laugh. Two jokes in

one night. "I suppose I'll have to keep you with me then," he joked back.

He smiled at her soft chuckle, then they reached the ladder leading up to the grate. Handing Liliana the lantern, he ascended first. The grate was in the middle of a street, but it was a sparsely traveled one. There was little likelihood of a carriage, or anything else, passing overhead, but he still felt compelled to make sure it was safe before inviting Liliana up.

Reaching the top of the ladder, he moved the heavy grate aside, sliding it across the cobblestones of the street. He peeked his head up to find nothing but waste bins and empty boxes lining the sides of the surrounding buildings.

"It's safe," he whispered down to her. "Blow out the lantern before you come up."

He hoisted himself out onto the street, then waited to retrieve the lantern from Liliana as she appeared. Soon the grate had been replaced, and the pair darted together through the shadows, toward the first meeting that would lead to the end of the *LN*, or so Arhyen hoped.

NOTE FROM THE AUTHOR

For news and updates, please join my mailing list by visiting:

www.saracroethle.com

Made in the USA
Middletown, DE
06 January 2018